SOLDIER BOY

a novel

DANNY RHODES

MAIA

Published in 2009 by
The Maia Press Limited
82 Forest Road
London E8 3BH
www.maiapress.com

Copyright © 2009 Danny Rhodes

ISBN 978 1 904559 36 8

A CIP catalogue record for this book is available
from the British Library

Printed and bound in Great Britain by Thanet Press
on paper from sustainable managed forests

Mixed Sources
Product group from well-managed
forests and other controlled sources
www.fsc.org Cert no. TT-COC-2023
© 1996 Forest Stewardship Council
FSC

For every mother's son

'Three strong men make a street'
Old Glasgow expression

Part One

1

Scottie and Drew were sheltering under the arches when the army trucks passed, five of them, one after another, muddy lads in uniform huddled in the back, tired faces staring blankly out of the darkness.

'Poor bastards,' said Drew. 'On a night like this.'

Scottie shrugged his shoulders.

'Serves them right,' he said.

'They'll not even see the game on TV.'

'Aye, but we'll be there.'

They were off to watch the Hoops. It was Tuesday, European night. Some side from Scandinavia was in for a hammering – it looked like half the city was on their way to witness it. Only the army trucks were heading away from the ground, heading up Hillside, red tail-lights flickering to nothing, the opposite carriageway full to bursting with headlights, cars and coaches, minibuses by the score, pavements on both sides flooded with people, all of them moving despite the rain, only Scottie and Drew staying put and all because of Mackie.

'He'll not leave us waiting much longer,' said Drew. 'If he does we'll just go without him.'

'Aye, and he'd better have cash with him,' said Scottie. 'These tickets cost a week's giro. Me mam'll go spare if she finds out.'

'I'll pay you Friday. I said I would.'

'I'm not talking about you, I'm talking about Mackie.'

'You'll be lucky,' said Drew. 'I said we'd be better just the two of us.'

'Yeah, but it's not the same without Mackie, is it? You know that.'

And it wasn't. That was the magic of it.

Half-time. The Hoops in command. Scottie wolfing down his hot-dog, reading the match programme over the shoulder of the bloke in front of him, Mackie and Drew chugging tea from plastic cups, enjoying their favourite game of 'predict the advert' on the electronic hoardings.

'363Bet.com,' said Mackie.

'Nah, Movie Channel,' said Drew.

They waited for the board to switch. 363 came up.

'Oh yes,' said Mackie. '1-0.'

'Lucky,' said Drew. 'Right, next one.'

'Hey, Scottie. You too!' said Mackie.

Scottie looked up from the programme.

'I'm eating this,' he said.

Mackie shrugged.

'Okay, Loans Direct,' said Scottie.

'PS2,' said Drew.

'You're both wrong. Vodafone,' said Mackie.

The three of them waited, staring at the hoardings, at 363.com, Mackie adding a drumroll with his tongue for good measure, blowing the steam from the tea up into the lights. When the next ad came up it read:

'Be the Best.'

'What's that for?' Mackie shouted.

'Army,' said Drew. 'I've seen the ad on TV.'

'Barmy army,' laughed Mackie.

'Barmy to join the army more like,' said Scottie. 'What a joke!'

After Scottie smashed the lad's face in he made his way to the school and broke in through a downstairs window. Snow was falling again, filling the sky with tiny flakes that moved in flurries on the breeze. The playground was covered in a fresh layer. It settled on the metal hoops of the basketball court, on the five-a-side goalposts and on the scrubby bushes below the bottom-floor windows. It settled on the second-floor windowsills too, and when Scottie slid one open the snow found its way into the classroom.

He watched the snow come down, felt some sort of calm descending with it. The rooftops of the estate were covered, the sky foggy pink, the houses white and shapeless. He fixed his eyes on the playground, checked the covering of snow for fresh tracks, signs that he'd missed something, signs that told him things were getting started at last. But there were no tracks. He couldn't even see the set he'd made an hour earlier, new snowfall only threatening then, his instincts carrying him onward, leading him to this place, telling him it was the thing to do, the best way of reminding everybody who he was and where he'd been, the best way to make them all sit up and take notice.

There were no spotlights outside, no white TV vans with satellite dishes on their roofs, no flashing blues, no megaphones, none of the things he'd expected. There was no siege, just him in a geography classroom without heating, faded maps on the walls, old textbooks he remembered from his days in the place piled on shelves, the sound of the wind whining, the sound of his own breath behind his muffler, the rifle resting against his good shoulder.

Downtown a lad was spreadeagled in the snow, blood seeping from his head, turning the snow pink, the blood darkening as it flowed. Scottie saw this in the last second before he ran, had the picture etched in his mind, couldn't get it out of there. It reminded him of the looter, but then everything reminded him of that event. He couldn't shake it from his being.

He slid the window shut and closed the night out, thought about leaving the school, heading back to his mam's, but it was too late for that. Besides, he'd done all he could. It hadn't made any difference. What he'd seen was his girlfriend in the arms of another lad, his mam inconsolable and his kid sister out of her head on drink. He didn't have it in him to go through any of that any more.

2

Months after leaving school, with nothing happening, Scottie, Mackie and Drew made their weekly trip to the job centre, down Hillside together against the morning traffic, three hunched grey ghosts, to the line of shops and the hairdresser's where Mel worked. Drew disappeared into the newsagent's while Scottie and Mackie waited outside on the pavement. Mackie tapped on the hairdresser's window. An old woman peered up at them from under a dryer and gave them a look. Mel was leaning on the counter reading a magazine. When she saw Scottie she came to the door.

'What are you doing?'

'We're going into town.'

'Yeah, well it's a good job the boss is out. She hates you lot hanging around outside.'

'We're not hanging around,' Scottie said. 'We're off to the Jobbie.'

'Off to the dole office more like,' said Mackie.

'You might be, but we're not.'

Mel put a hand on Scottie's shoulder and pulled him towards her. She spoke quietly into his ear.

'I'm not being funny. I just don't want to get in trouble again. It's not you.'

'I know,' said Scottie. 'I told him not to do it but you know what he's like. I'll see you later, yeah?'

She kissed him once and then went back inside. Scottie watched her explain herself to the old woman then turned to Mackie.

'You're a real prat. Do you know that?'

Mackie laughed.

'She was hardly busy, propped up with that magazine.'

'She's just training,' said Scottie. 'You've no idea.'

'I know you don't train by sitting at the counter reading magazines.'

'You have to start somewhere.'

'It's like what Andy told me about the call centre. All you have to do is answer the phone and take an order. How can it take a month to learn that? I've no patience for it.'

'Just don't tap on the window,' said Scottie. 'She gets into trouble.'

'Why?' asked Mackie. 'It's me that's doing the tapping.'

'That's not . . .'

Scottie stopped talking. There was no point with Mackie sometimes. He wouldn't listen. He'd been like it all the way through school, driving the teachers crazy, having an answer to everything that was said. With Mackie, the best thing to do was leave things hanging.

'It doesn't matter,' Scottie said in the end. 'Just don't tap on the window.'

They carried on down Hillside, passing the cemetery, the sky muddy, the gravestones on the other side of the railings damp and mottled.

'Did you hear about those kids from the north estate?' Mackie asked.

Scottie and Drew shook their heads.

'They broke into one of those posh monument things and opened up the coffin inside. There was a body in it.'

'Mackie . . .' Scottie started.

'No, listen,' said Mackie. 'It was mental. They nicked the head off this corpse and started scaring all the oldies with it. Mental.'

Mackie started running around, pretending he was carrying the thing.

'It's not funny,' said Scottie. 'It's sick.'

'Then why are you laughing? See? See? It's funny. It was a hundred years old. It wasn't like it was someone's grandma or anything.'

'Still sick,' said Drew.

'What's wrong with you two today? You're a couple of boring farts.'

'I'm sick of having no money,' said Scottie. 'That's what's wrong with me.'

'You'll get something today,' said Mackie. 'There's always something, even if it's nothing.'

'I'm not interested in nothing,' said Scottie.

Their old school was set back off the road at the foot of the hill. Scottie stared at the steamed-up windows as they passed, at the shadowy forms of the kids inside, kids desperate to be where he was now, outside looking in. They didn't know the half of it.

Eleven in the morning, six or seven girls huddled together by the wall beyond the gate, smoking, sharing drags and laughing. Scottie's sister was one of them.

'Shouldn't you be inside?' Scottie asked her.

'Dunno,' she said. 'Shouldn't you be at work?'

The other girls laughed.

'I thought you told Mam you'd quit smoking,' Scottie shouted.

'I thought you told Mam you were going to get a job,' shouted Claire.

Mackie laughed.

'You'd best get to lessons before Mam heads this way,' Scottie said.

His sister shot him the finger and blew a train of smoke into the air.

She shouted to Drew.

'See you later, Mr Cleaning Man.'

Drew shook his head.

'See?' he said. 'It's not worth it. All I get is grief. Last night they had me going at chewing gum on the stairs!'

'I bet it was Claire's, trying to freshen her breath,' said Mackie. 'All ready to give you one.'

Scottie punched him on the arm.

'Shut it,' he said. 'She's still my sister.'

'Oh yeah, I forgot,' Mackie said. 'Little Miss Innocent.'

'There's no way I'm going back there,' said Drew.

'At least it's something,' said Scottie. 'At least it pays for your driving lessons.'

'Aye,' said Drew. 'That's the only good thing about it. The kids just take the piss.'

'We used to take the piss when we were there. Remember Wilkinson? You were forever giving it to him.'

'It's not the same.'

'Just because you're on the receiving end,' said Mackie.

'No. They mean it. They're nasty. We were just having a laugh. We were never nasty.'

'Mate, you're getting old,' said Mackie. 'Next thing we know you'll be sorting your pension!'

'He'll be getting meals on wheels brought to the shed,' said Scottie.

It was forever the same, a never-ending cycle, one of the three always on the receiving end. When there was a lull each of them jockeyed for position before the next round began, sometimes Mackie versus the other two, sometimes Scottie, sometimes Drew, never a true moment existing where all three sat equal, never a moment's respite.

He had run through the snow until he reached the school, smashed the window with the rifle butt, climbed through the space and pushed two sets of lockers in front of the hole to block it. Then he'd made his way upstairs to the top floor, his footsteps hollow in the empty stairwell, his breath showing in the freezing corridors, his whole body aching. He chose the classroom on the corner because it had the best arc of fire, just like they'd trained him to do, and then he slumped to the floor underneath the windows and pulled the muffler to his face.

He'd come a long way, thousands of miles across land and air and sea. He'd come all that way with half a shoulder missing to find out his girlfriend didn't want to know him any more. His city didn't want to know him either. He wasn't the same person as the one who'd left.

It didn't take a genius to work that out.

3

The job centre was crowded, the air stale. The three of them went in together but after five minutes spent gazing at the boards Mackie was through with it.

'I hate this place. I'll wait for you outside,' he said.

It was all the same stuff – labouring work, the call centres up on the new business park or the chicken factory. Everything else was out of reach.

'Mate, I'm gonna have to try the chicken place,' said Drew. 'If I spend another day in that school I'll lose it.'

'No way,' said Scottie. 'I'm sticking to signing on.'

'How long is it going to be before they shove you up there for an interview? They're bound to sooner or later.'

'I'll just tell them I'm not interested. Tell them I've got skills.'

'What skills?'

'I don't know. Any skills. What about driving jobs? What do I need for those?'

'It's all twenty-one and over. It's the insurance. Besides, you'll not be driving for ages.'

'I'm well stitched up,' said Scottie. 'Sometimes I think Mackie's got the right idea.'

'They'll catch up with him,' said Drew. 'They'll stop his money if he keeps this up.'

When they turned, Mackie was outside the window, pulling faces at the glass.

'He's pathetic sometimes,' said Drew. 'Like a kid.'

Mackie saw they were talking about him and gave them the same finger Scottie's sister had. One of the job centre clerks noticed they were with him.

'Can you ask your friend to go away?' she said.

'You ask him,' said Drew. 'He's nothing to do with us.'

Drew turned to Scottie.

'See? He needs sorting out. I'm sick of him making us look stupid.'

Scottie looked back at the window. Mackie was sat with his back against the glass now, fiddling with his mobile.

'He's got no credit,' said Drew. 'He's just playing solitaire and hoping someone'll text him. Then when they do he'll ask to borrow one of ours to send a message back.'

'You've got to love him,' said Scottie.

Drew shrugged.

'I just wish he'd have a go at sorting his life out,' he said.

'Like us you mean?' asked Scottie.

'At least we're in here, mate,' said Drew. 'At least we're trying.'

Scottie let his eyes float around the place. He felt his heart sink. This was everything he'd been warned against. It was as if every character and event in the stories he'd had to endure from his teachers since he was thirteen years old had converged on this moment, and the moment was laughing at him. He walked around between the boards, dismissing each and every card, waiting for the bloke on the desk to call his name.

As it turned out, it was the bloke on the desk who told them about the army recruiting day.

'You may as well take a look,' he said. 'It ticks a box on your form to say you're trying.'

Drew was all for it.

'Go on Scottie. Stick our names down. Hey, let's stick Mackie's down too.'

Scottie looked over to the window. Mackie was still sat out there with his back against it. It'd be worth it just to see his face when they told him.

'Can you fit us in this morning?' asked Scottie.

'Not till half-past one,' said the bloke. He checked his watch.

'Okay then,' Scottie told him. 'Stick me down.'

'Me too,' said Drew. 'We've got a mate . . .'

'Sorry, lads,' said the bloke. 'They're not here to waste time. If your mate's interested send him in.'

They went to the chippie to kill the hours. Drew and Scottie sat on the steps outside the place, digging into a pile, Mackie with no chips buzzing around them, unable to settle.

'The army!' said Mackie. 'Are you mental?'

'It's just to tick a box,' said Scottie. 'You have to prove you're looking.'

'Yeah, but the army! No way, mate, all those tossers ordering you around. I've seen that *Bad Lads' Army* on the telly.'

'It won't be like that,' said Drew.

'We're only having a quick interview to keep the bloke in there quiet,' said Scottie. 'I'm not signing anything.'

'Give us a chip then,' said Mackie.

'Piss off and get your own.'

'What with?'

'Exactly. If you stuck a job for more than five minutes you'd have enough to get some.'

'Like you, you mean?'

'I'm waiting for something that's worth doing.'

'Like getting yourself killed?'

'I already told you, I'm not signing up. It's just for the records, to keep them in there happy.'

Scottie fished in his pocket for a quid and let Mackie go and get his own. When he came out he had a piece of fish to go with it.

'Where did you get that?'

'Jimmy's about to shut. I told him it wasn't any good to anybody in the bin so he chucked it in my bag.'

'You're a jammy bastard.'

'I'm an opportunist, my friend. It's survival of the fittest.'

'Give us some then.'

'No way. Go and get your own.'

Mackie joined them on the steps, and there they sat, the three lads from Calton, mates since primary school. They knew each other inside out, knew each other's weak points and knew each other's strengths, but the fun was in prodding at the weak points, prising open defences, getting a shot in before the tables were turned.

The two army blokes were a laugh. They didn't ask Scottie any questions to catch him out and they weren't interested with how he'd got on at school.

'Do you drive?' the first one asked.

Scottie shook his head.

'Not yet,' he said.

'You can take your test with the army,' said the officer. 'All at Her Majesty's expense. How are you with travel?'

Scottie shrugged.

'Not done much of it.'

The second officer smiled.

'In the army you get to travel. Canada, Germany, Switzerland. Ever skied? Done any mountaineering? Fancy it? Well, this is your chance.'

It sounded all right.

'What about pay?' Scottie asked.

'Straight down to business,' said the first officer. 'I like that. It's probably more than you think. You're looking at £260 a week starting out and remember, no bills in that, no rent, meals provided.'

Scottie couldn't contain a grin. £260 a week. That was

five times what he got on the social and he was paying his mam rent on what he got now. He'd be a millionaire.

'How does it all work then?' he asked.

Scottie's last interview had been at the builder's yard on the industrial estate. It was drizzling with rain when he'd turned up. The boss was late so he'd had to sit on the wall out front and wait, drowning in it. He watched the cars heading into town, wondering what he was doing there and what he was going to say. Eventually, a silver BMW pulled up. The boss was short, bald, busy and had no time for chit-chat. While Scottie stood in a shallow puddle of water in the yard the boss told him what the hours were, how he didn't accept lateness or laziness.

'It's manual labour. You ever done any hod-carrying?'

Scottie shook his head but pushed his chest out, trying to show the bloke how big he was. The boss looked him up and down.

'Take a day off sick because you can't be arsed to come in and there won't be a job when you turn up the next morning. Storm off in a strop because the brickies are taking the piss out of you and there won't be a job when you turn up the next morning,' he said. 'Anyway, where are you from?'

'I was born here,' said Scottie.

'Yeah, funny. I mean where do you live?'

'Hillside,' Scottie said.

The boss stared him up and down again.

'Got a criminal record?'

Scottie shook his head again.

'Sure?'

'Yeah.'

The boss chewed on his lip.

'I've got three other lads like you to see. Leave your number and I'll get back to you.'

After that the boss disappeared into an old mobile unit that reminded Scottie of school. He didn't call that day or the next. Scottie's mam told him to call instead and show some willing. She said it might make all the difference. Scottie thought about it but in the end he didn't bother. There was no point and anyway he wasn't interested.

He had a couple of other interviews that were the same. One was at a corner store where they wanted him to work every Friday and Saturday on the late shift. He thought about how that would be, working late shifts on weekends, dealing with the pissed-up lads who came in for munchies, lads that knew him from school, clearing up the puke and taking abuse for the sake of a few quid a week extra. He thought about how Mel would react to him losing his weekends. The job was a joke when you added it all up. The other was at a car-wash. That was going okay until they found out he wasn't eighteen. He had to be eighteen to work the machinery. They told him to come and see them when he was old enough.

'What do you have to do?' Mackie said when Scottie told him. 'Point a hose at a hub-cap, mop a few windscreens.'

'Something to do with Health and Safety,' said Scottie.

'How much were they paying?' asked Mackie.

'They didn't say. Fiver an hour. Something like that.'

'That's the same as the store.'

'Forget it. I'm not doing weekends or late shifts.'

'It's the chicken factory then.'

They looked at each other and spoke at the same time.

'I'm not working at the chicken factory.'

It got them laughing. Mackie started making clucking noises, prancing in circles around the place. He was doing it when Drew turned up at the shed with a six-pack of lager and the latest ripped Bond movie for them to watch. Drew took one look at Mackie's antics and shrugged his shoulders as if there was nothing Mackie could do any more that might surprise him.

The officers talked him through it all, how he'd have to sign up for four years, how he'd have to pass a medical, how basic training and infantry training worked.

'Do you think you're tough enough?' asked the first officer.

Scottie nodded.

'I reckon.'

'Are you fit?'

'I'm okay.'

'Can you run?'

'I used to do okay at school,' said Scottie and he kicked himself inside, for mentioning school, for bringing it up. They were sure to ask him now.

But they didn't.

'We're looking for lads that are tough, fit, reliable, adaptable, determined and loyal.'

'Is that all?' asked Scottie. 'Sounds a breeze.'

The first officer laughed.

'And the lad's got a sense of humour, too. Good. You'll go a long way.'

They explained what he'd have to do to get himself ready for the entrance test.

'It's mainly upper-body work and aerobic fitness. And the common sense you've got up here, that counts too.' The officer pointed towards his temple. 'If you've got anything about you it'll be a doddle.'

Scottie got up to leave, barely containing the way he was feeling.

'How old are you?' asked the second officer.

'Seventeen,' said Scottie.

'You're a big lad for seventeen. Ever boxed?'

Scottie shook his head.

'You will,' said the officer. 'And if you're seventeen you're going to need parental permission to join.'

'My dad's away,' said Scottie.

'Right. What about your mum?'

'Yeah. There is me mam.'

Scottie looked at the floor.

'Every soldier needs a mum,' said the officer.

Scottie smiled but he was thinking about his mam, about how he was going to tell her and what she might say to him when he did.

'No worries then,' said the first officer. 'We'll set up a date for you to do the course. It'll be a weekend. We'll send you a letter.'

Scottie got up to leave but as he did the officers got up too. They met him at the door and each of them shook his hand. For the first time in years Scottie felt different about himself. He wouldn't have been able to explain it if anybody asked him but the feeling was there all the same. He felt it when he stepped out into the street. The wind struck him in the chest and face but he felt bigger and stronger against it than when he'd gone in the place. There was a poster in the window of the job centre showing an army lad scaling a wall. Scottie felt he could step over the wall without breaking stride.

'Hark at you,' said Mackie.

'What?' Scottie asked.

'You're gonna do it. I can see it in your eyes.'

Scottie grinned.

'It's not so bad,' he said. '£260 a week.'

'You're mental,' said Mackie. 'Real mental.'

They waited under the canopy until Drew came out.

'What do you reckon?' he asked.

'What do *you* reckon?' asked Scottie. Then they grinned at each other.

'You've both lost it,' said Mackie, but neither of them were listening to him. Their heads were swelling to the point of bursting.

That afternoon Scottie and Drew were full of the army, talk-ing about driving tests and cars, the money they'd be getting. Mackie kept his distance and said nothing. At the travel agent's a poster of a tanned blonde in a bikini beckoned them over.

'Imagine meeting her for real,' said Drew.

They checked out the cheap deals in the window.

'Ibiza, boys, that's where we want to be,' said Mackie. 'Look at that. It's dirt cheap.'

'Listen to you,' said Scottie. 'How are you going to find the cash?'

'If we're going I can get it,' said Mackie. 'Let's do it. We'll get a last-minute thing.'

'We'll do it next year,' said Drew. 'We'll all go together after training's finished.'

'There won't be a next year,' said Mackie.

4

The next Monday morning saw Scottie trudging up Hillside towards the business park. He was following the smell, his legs carrying him towards their destination while his mind drifted somewhere else. He'd heard nothing from the army so the job centre had set him up with an interview at the chicken factory. Each time he looked up the factory grew bigger until finally, inexplicably, he was standing in reception with the others, hating himself and hating them, hating the woman on the desk for the way she spoke to him, like he was brainless, the way she looked at him, simply hating every single thing, the stink, the furniture, the colour of the carpet. A man came out and introduced himself. He was carrying a clipboard. He started ticking their names off one by one. Half of them were foreign. Scottie didn't get everything he said. He was too busy looking at the others, wondering where they came from and what they were doing here, if they were like him, hating it or looking forward to getting on. He wondered how that could be possible.

Clipboard man led them through a set of doors and down a corridor. It was clean, spotless even, but it wasn't presentable like the reception. There was no public face here. It just was. They ended up in a white room with a long table at its centre. There were twelve places set, one place for each of them and on the table in front of each chair was a folder with the company name and the words 'health and safety' printed on the front and if the world had ended then, in that moment, with no warning, Scottie would have welcomed it, because he knew what was coming, what the next three hours of his life were going to be like and he almost turned around and walked out. But he couldn't. He had to earn the right not to come back. He had to show willing, even if the job was crap, even if the place was for the drongoes on the estate, the ones who were already looking at the folders, some wide-eyed like they'd never seen anything like it before, others with trepidation in case they were about to be asked to read it.

Scottie sat down in the chair nearest to him. A middle-aged woman tried to smile at him but he didn't give her the chance to make eye contact. Clipboard man was talking again, something about page numbers but already it was clear that at least three of the group weren't listening to a word he was saying. Scottie was one of them. He flicked the corner of the folder open and let it drop, flicked it open, let it drop until clipboard man looked at him and repeated his instruction about page numbers. This time Scottie got him. He turned to page three, as instructed, and caught the contents page. Rows of headings and sub-headings stared back at him. His heart sank so far into his chest that he had to physically fight to draw breath. After that the minutes creaked by, each one pulling and dragging the next one after it and each minute fighting harder than the last to get away, not to be consigned to a fate such as this, to be wasted like this, lost, forgotten or, worse, to be remembered and hated for eternity.

For lunch they ate triangular-cut sandwiches and drank orange juice from plastic beakers, then they were led further into the factory, into the guts of the place, where the workers stood in rows at tables and conveyor belts. One hour on, fifteen minutes off, one hour on, fifteen minutes off, around the clock, in time with the clock, a part of the clock, part of its rhythm. Scottie stood stock-still, taking it all in. It was right there in front of him, his life for the next forty years if he wanted it. The money would be okay. It wasn't great but okay for what it was. It was secure and it was protected. It would provide. And he could change jobs, change from one processing operation to another, with promotion always on the cards for somebody with a bit about them, if he wanted it, if he really, really wanted it. But the place would turn him into a machine, or bits of a machine at least, extract vital parts of him or render them inactive. He could feel it happening already, parts of his brain switching to manual, realising they'd not be needed here. The place would swallow him eventually, spit him out with a pension and a load of stories about the people who'd passed through one end and out of the other. There would still be the weekends, four weeks holiday a year, Christmas parties, birthday and retirement celebrations. There'd be babies and weddings and affairs. It was almost a life.

At the end of the tour, while clipboard man was still talking about prospects and career paths and certificates, Scottie turned and made his way towards the sunlight beyond reception, not stopping to sign out, not even looking at the receptionist. True enough, it was almost a life, but it wasn't ever going to be his life.

When he stepped out into the afternoon he was actually glad he'd been inside the place. The experience had cemented his thoughts. By the time he reached the edge of the car park he was breaking into a run. It didn't matter that he was in trousers and a shirt with a collar, it didn't matter that he was wearing his best shoes. He picked up speed, accelerated with each step until he was sprinting through the business park, back towards Hillside, his legs driving him forward, his feet hardly touching the ground. At home he called Drew and shouted into the phone when he answered,

'I'm doing it! Do you hear me? I'm doing it!'

And before Drew could say a word he'd slammed the phone down again, was out of the shirt, out of his shoes, out in the yard slamming press-ups into the earth, right there underneath his mam's washing line, one, two, three, four, five. His mam came out and watched him, watched her son doing press-ups in just his old school trousers, the sweat forming in the small of his back, his arms pumping, his breath shooting out.

'How did it go?' she asked. 'What did you think?'

He stopped at the bottom of a rep, held himself there and tilted his head towards her.

'Oh,' she said. 'I think I get it.'

Then she turned and went back inside.

He stayed out there, sixty-one, sixty-two, sixty-three until he got past eighty and then he collapsed to the ground, muscles burning, froth and spittle coming out of his mouth. People in the alley might have thought he was dead, might have seen his body there and thought his heart had exploded in his chest, but they'd have been wrong. He was more alive than he'd ever been. For the first time, he knew where life was taking him.

Back in the house, his mam was busy at the sink. He grabbed a pint glass from the cupboard and moved alongside her, trying to get to the tap.

'You're sure about this?' she asked.

He filled the glass with water, let it overflow over his fingers, waiting for it to run ice cold.

'Aye,' he said. 'One hundred per cent.'

'Well, if you know what you're doing,' she said.

He twisted the tap shut and drank the water down in large gulps, not stopping for air.

'It's dangerous,' she said. 'It's not all fun and games.'

He put the glass down on the drainer, wiped his lips with the back of his arm.

'One hundred per cent,' he said again.

'It's your decision, I suppose,' his mam said. 'But speak to Uncle Jack about it first, won't you? Just to hear what he has to say?'

Scottie nodded.

'I was going to do that anyway,' he said, then he went upstairs to get a shower, leaving her staring out of the window at the washing line and the patch of worn ground beneath it.

The army letters came three days later. Drew brought his over to the shed and they read through them together, munching on Chinese takeaway.

'Medical and selection course,' said Drew. 'What do you reckon we'll have to do?'

'It'll be all that stuff they did at school,' said Scottie. 'You know, listening to your chest, pants down and cough . . .'

The two of them looked at each other and laughed. Drew spat a chicken ball into the packet.

'No way,' he said.

'Do you want to go and check out that website?' Scottie asked him.

'Aye, we'd better,' said Drew.

They used Drew's mam's computer. The questions asked them how they felt about life, how they felt about themselves, what they liked to do in their spare time, what sort of job they might like to do, loads of other stuff like that. All they had to do was click and move on to the next question. At the end of the test they got a profile and a colour to guide them. There were four colours, *red, blue, green* and *amber,* and each one said a different thing about the person they were. Drew went first. He rushed through the test, clicking on pictures of cash and girls whenever he could, laughing all the way through and saying things like, 'I'll have a bit of that.'

At the end he came out *amber*. *Amber* meant he was look-ing to make changes in his life. It also said he was unsure about stuff and that he'd lost direction. He stopped reading after that.

'These things are crap,' he said. 'Lost direction. What's that all about?'

He went off to get himself some more grub, left Scottie at the computer.

Scottie took his time with it. Each time a question came up he read it carefully and then looked at *all* of the pictures, trying to make sure he chose the one that suited him, the one that said the most about him and the person he was.

He shouted down the stairs to Drew.

'Green, mate. Team player. It says the army's built around people like me!'

Drew shouted back, 'Big deal.'

Scottie went back to the computer. The thing that told him how he viewed his life now was spot on. It said he was somebody who valued his mates and that he'd stick with them through thick and thin. It said he was uncertain about the future, which was exactly how he felt, but that he'd be okay if he had people there to help him. It said the army could do that.

After that he clicked on the jobs and put 'green' into the box that asked him what sort of a person he was. A list of jobs came up. Most of them were infantry. That was okay. That was exactly what he wanted. Scottie grinned to himself. He couldn't help it. It was like the army knew him. It had been like that with the officers in the job centre and it was like that on the website, like the whole thing was meant to be. He felt something lurch in his stomach. He hadn't felt anything like it since he'd first got together with Mel.

5

'You're not going to church with your mam then?'

Sunday morning. Scottie and Mel curled up together in bed at her place. Bells pealing outside.

'That was just to get her off my back.'

'She's still on about it?'

'She's always on about it, always dropping hints, so I thought I'd try a different tactic and call her bluff. That's why I went the last few times.'

'Did it work?'

Mel looked him in the eye.

'You're joking, right?'

He shrugged.

'Of course it didn't work. She'll be knocking in a minute and when I say I'm not going she'll be off in a huff. She won't stop going on about it until she gets her way and I'm there every single week. I suppose you could come with me . . .'

'Yeah, right,' Scottie said.

'Why not? It'd put a smile on her face.'

'It'd be too weird. You were brought up with it. I haven't been to church since I was a kid. And anyway, when you're dead you're dead.'

'Shut up,' said Mel.

'Why?'

'Think those things if you want but don't say them.'

'In case your mam hears me?'

'My mam's the way she is because of my dad. You know that.'

'I remember seeing them when I was off to play footy. I remember his wheelchair.'

'He hated that thing.'

A silence.

'You know there was never a time when my dad tried to force the church on me. My mam goes on about how he'd turn in his grave and all that but it's not true. He said I'd come to it when I was ready if I came to it at all.'

She stopped again, then smiled that smile, her mischievous smile, again.

'Course if we want a church wedding we'll both have to go a few times. Together.'

'You in white,' Scottie said. 'What a joke that'd be . . .'

'I can soon change that,' she said.

'What's done is done,' said Scottie.

'Doesn't mean I can't make a bit more effort. Just until the big day. When was it going to be again? Two years? Three?'

'Ha ha,' Scottie said. 'You'd never last.'

'Try me,' she said.

'That's blackmail,' he laughed.

She shrugged. He went to kiss her but she turned away, hopped off the bed.

'Once a Catholic always a Catholic,' Scottie whispered.

'You're Catholic too.'

'But I don't think about it.'

'Why are you whispering?' Mel giggled.

'In case she's listening,' said Scottie.

'Why would she be listening?'

'She's always listening.'

Hours ticked by. He didn't feel much about the lad he'd hit, only that he'd got together with Mel, chased and chased her even though he knew who Scottie was and why he was away, chased her until she caved in. So he'd got what he deserved in the end. He didn't feel sorry for Mel either because she'd let herself cave in, hadn't put up much of a fight, not the sort of fight that three years deserved, not the sort of fight you put up for the person you loved who was off defending the freedoms of your country. She'd caved in so he'd caved the lad's face in. Fair was fair.

They came out of the club together, see, locked arm in arm, him all over her. They were so into each other they didn't even notice him when he stepped out of the shadows. Mel looked Scottie in the eye and then walked right past him, like he didn't exist, like everything they'd shared had never happened, so he shoved the butt of the rifle into the lad's face and knocked him to the ground. That got their attention. Mel started screaming then. Screaming like the looter had screamed.

People came, converging on the scene until they saw how crazy he was and what he was carrying, then they changed their minds. They couldn't get out of there fast enough. He heard one shout, 'Some squaddie's lost it.'

They didn't have a clue. They'd not been where he'd been and they'd not seen what he'd seen.

He put the heel of his boot on the lad's face and looked at Mel. The lad was scrabbling around at his feet, trying to get away, trying to get up and hold his broken nose all at the same time but Scottie was only interested in Mel's eyes, to see what she was about to do next, to see where her loyalties lay. When she screamed at him to stop and started swinging away at him, not caring about the danger she was in, when she did that and looked at him like he was a piece of dirt, with no feeling or connection, then he knew it was over. He shoved her away, just with his hands, stuck the boot in on the lad some more and legged it, kicking up the virgin snow just like the dust and sand in the desert.

6

'**What's that** supposed to mean?' Scottie asked.

They were lying together on the sofa in the shed, watching *Coronation Street*, Mel on the inside snug and warm, Scottie tipping over the edge each time he moved. They were talking about the army.

'Nothing,' said Mel.

Scottie turned his eyes from the TV to Mel and then back to the TV again.

'You've said it now. You may as well tell me what you mean.'

'I didn't mean anything,' said Mel. 'I was just saying, that's all.'

'Saying that I'm useless,' said Scottie.

'No. If I thought that I wouldn't be with you.'

'What then? Heard what before?'

She sat up, causing him to slip off the sofa again. He had to put a foot down hard to steady himself.

'I just meant that I'm not going to think too much about this army thing before you go ahead and take the medical. You've got two weeks to change your mind . . .'

'And?'

'And knowing you, you'll change it, like you have all the other times.'

'What other times?'

She held out a hand and started counting off fingers.

'College. Mechanic apprenticeship. Trainee plumber. Re-sits.'

'I never said I was going to do any re-sits.'

'You thought about it, when they wouldn't take you as a mechanic.'

Scottie sat himself up away from her.

'This is different,' he said.

He pointed a finger at her.

'It's all right for you. You walk out of school and Maureen says you can start at the shop.'

'I've been talking about it since year ten at school. I was working there when we started going out.'

'You think I'm a useless bastard,' he said.

She tried to look him in the eye but he wasn't having it.

'I don't think you're useless,' she said. 'I just want to see you sorted. So we can do more things together.'

'So what *do* you think?' he asked her.

'How long would you be away for?'

'When?'

'If they take you.'

'I'm not sure. Me and Drew are going to find out more tomorrow.'

She reached out and took hold of his hand, pulled him back on to the sofa next to her.

'Would you miss me?' she asked.

'Yeah,' he said. 'Would you miss me?'

'Of course,' she said.

She smiled to herself but in a way that he could see.

'What?' he asked.

'Would you have a uniform?'

He blushed and grinned at the same time.

'You're bad,' he said.

'That's why you love me.'

She rolled underneath him, pinched his arms.

'Feel that puppy fat,' she said, giggling.

'Give me six months,' he said. 'You'll see the difference.'

Afterwards, the two of them pressed into the sofa like they were part of it, Mel whispered in his ear, still away with sleep.

'Just say this isn't going to be like the other times.'

'It isn't,' he whispered back. 'It feels different. It feels like something that's already happening, not something that'll never happen.'

He lay beside her, staring at the flickering TV. The volume was down. A panel of suits were taking questions, some bloke in the audience getting agitated, his face flushed. People were applauding him, others trying to shout him down. It looked like things were about to kick off but it wasn't his type of thing so he turned it off. He lay in darkness instead, feeling Mel's breath on his neck, feeling her heart beat, thinking things through. She was making a real go of the hairdressing, hadn't had a day off sick since she started. He was well proud of her for what she was doing and he owed it to her to make something happen. He owed it to himself, too.

7

Waiting for Drew to turn up, munching on his second burger of the morning, Scottie stood staring at a sky full of dark clouds. Heavy droplets of rain had just begun to fall. He watched the first few splatter against the window and thought about giving the whole thing a miss. They could do it tomorrow or the day after that, wait for a day when the sun was shining. There was no rush.

Drew appeared at the gate, kitted up in his sports gear. Coming down the path he noticed Scottie, pointed to the heavens and swore. Scottie went to the door to let him in.

'It's gonna spew it down, said Drew.

'Aye,' Scottie said.

Drew's eyes fell on the burger.

'You're not eating that before,' he said.

'My second one,' said Scottie.

'You're mad. Forget the rain, you'll be chucking your guts up before we get to the end of the street.'

'You need your scoff if you're gonna run. Where do you think you get your energy from?'

'Aye, but not just before,' said Drew. 'It won't even have a chance to go down.'

Scottie bit into the burger. A drop of tomato sauce fell out of it and landed on his Hoops shirt, right in the middle of his chest.

'Aw . . .'

Drew laughed. Scottie went to the sink and started wiping at the shirt with the dishcloth. Pretty soon there was a wet, red stain all the way down the front of him.

'Join the army?' said Drew. 'You'll be lucky to get in the cub scouts.'

Scottie pointed at Drew.

'Says you in your perfect whites. Don't tell me your mam didn't get those sparkling.'

He threw the cloth in the sink.

'Sod it,' he said. 'I'm wearing it anyway.'

'Are you sure you want to go now?'

Bigger drops were landing, running away down the glass.

Scottie thought about the night before with Mel, the way she'd looked at him when he'd told her his master plan.

'We'll not have a choice on the day,' Scottie said. 'Besides, the rain'll keep us cool.'

And so they stepped out into it, Scottie slamming the door behind him.

'We must be mental,' said Drew.

'Mackie says we are,' said Scottie.

'Who cares what he thinks?' said Drew. 'Come on.'

They started at the gate, taking it easy, winding their way along the paths and alleys of the estate. There were so many nooks and crannies it was hard to get moving. A gang of kids in hoodies shouted at them, pointed and laughed and two women in a window shot them a wolf-whistle. They both started laughing as they ran, but by the time they were up on Hillside their smiles were drained and they were both concentrating on nothing but the running. They were up towards the cemetery when the heavens opened for real. Great drops fell then, splattering their faces, bare arms, knees, but they were into hard running now and it didn't matter. They searched for a rhythm instead. When they passed the row of shops and the hairdresser's the most Scottie did was turn his head to see if

Mel would see him but she was over by the till with her back to the window, busy at something. He was angry for that because he wanted her to know he was serious about it.

The two of them kept it together, running in step, their trainers slapping the pavement in tandem, slapping down into the puddles that were forming, slapping on the concrete and the paving stones, the gravel, the grass verges. Scottie's eyes were stinging where his hair gel had run down his forehead.

'That'll be history soon,' laughed Drew. 'They'll shave the lot off.'

'Nah, they only do that in the movies,' said Scottie.

They stopped at the top of the park, running on the spot under the branches of the big trees, sheltering the best they could, Scottie rubbing his eyes in an effort to wash the pain away. Water fell from the leaves and ran down their necks, causing them to swear at each other, each one breathing from deep within himself, breathing hard and heavy.

'You okay?' asked Scottie.

'Aye,' said Drew. 'Why wouldn't I be?'

'I was thinking about your chest.'

Drew took another breath. There was a moment where Scottie thought he shouldn't have said it. A different kind of silence to the one they had shared when they were running sat between them for a few seconds. Then Drew looked him in the eye.

'No worries,' he said. 'I've got control of it. Come on!'

They moved off again, around the edge of the park, keeping to the path, dodging the deeper puddles, along the ridge and back down again, back out on to Hillside, back past the row of shops and Mel who caught a glimpse of them this time and came to the window with a look on her face.

'Did you see that?' said Drew. 'What a picture!'

Scottie smiled inwardly. He'd show her. One way or another she'd see that he could start something – and finish it.

'How's that?' Drew asked when they reached the gate.

Scottie looked at the clock on the kitchen wall.

'Not bad,' he said. 'We'll have to knock off some more time to be sure though.'

'Okay,' said Drew.

'Same again tomorrow,' said Scottie. 'And the day after and the day after that.'

'Easy,' said Drew.

But they were both gasping.

Inside they downed a pint of water each and watched the rain fall like there was no tomorrow. The back yard was flooding, puddles forming in the wells of earth that had once been a lawn, long, long ago when Scottie's father had been around, back in the days when he bothered to keep it in order.

'Jesus, look at it. What a couple of twats.'

'I bet you nearly puked up those burgers,' said Drew.

'No way,' said Scottie. 'They're long gone. I'm about ready for another.'

'You're not right,' said Drew. 'You never have been.'

Burgers in fists, they went out to the shed and stuck daytime TV on, the rain still hammering down on the roof. Scottie had to put the bucket out where the leak was. His uncle would have fixed it, would have known exactly what to do and how to do it, but his uncle was not his old self these days and his mam was worried about him. Still, it was only a leak in weather like this. It wasn't the end of the world.

Scottie flicked the channel, flicked it again and again but there was nothing except rubbish and repeats of rubbish. In the end they stuck a Hoops DVD on and crashed out, Scottie on the sofa, Drew on the bottom bunk.

'Wake me when it stops raining,' said Drew.

Scottie belched from the burger.

'I'm gonna make another,' Scottie said. 'Do you want one?'

Drew shook his head in disbelief.

'See what I mean?' he asked.

'I know you do,' said Scottie. 'I'll make you one of me specials.'

8

When Scottie's alarm went off it was still dark outside. He hit the snooze button and rolled over in his bed, wrapping himself deeper into the covers, desperate to drag things out for a few more minutes. The next thing he knew the alarm was raging again. This time he got himself up. He heard his mam clattering around. She made him tea and toast and when he complained he could do it himself she was having none of it.

'It's what mams are for. You'll be wishing you had me there with you in a few weeks.'

'I've to get in first,' said Scottie.

'You'll get in,' she said. 'They'd be mad not to take you.'

Upstairs, a piece of toast between his teeth, he finished packing his bag, threw his trainers and Hoops shirt in, some spare boxers and socks. All the while he was thinking about the test, thinking how it could go wrong, how he might have to come home with his tail between his legs, fit for nothing but the chicken factory after all. He didn't have any deodorant left so he sneaked into the bathroom and nicked Terry's. He stuffed it down into the side pocket with his toothbrush and toothpaste, chucked in his aftershave and zipped the bag shut. That was it. He didn't bother with his hair gel for fear of one of the lads taking the piss. He was only going for a night and it wasn't a fashion parade.

He said bye to his mam and stepped out into the morning then stopped at the gate for a second to calm himself. The curtains in his sister's window were closed. A thin film of condensation covered the glass. Dawn was breaking on the estate. It was foggy and the air was wet with it. Everything was still. He didn't see anybody, just a cat on a doorstep. It ducked down low when it spotted him and watched him until he turned the corner. Then it was just him and the whine and clink of a milk truck making its way up Hillside.

Drew was waiting outside the row of shops where Mel worked. They caught the bus into the city then made their way on foot to the Recruiting Office. They didn't say much. Scottie's thoughts were stuck on the things Mel had said. He kept thinking about what he was going to do if they didn't take him, how he was going to face her and what she'd say. There was no reason for it. It was just that he was like that. He'd come to expect rejection.

There were four lads waiting outside the recruiting office, all but one with a bag slung over their shoulder or at their feet. Three of them were bunched together and chatting. They nodded at Scottie and Drew. The other lad was separated from the rest. He was thin and paler-skinned than any of the others. All he had was a plastic shopping bag. Scottie could see the soles of a scabby pair of trainers through the plastic. There wasn't a sign of much else.

The pick-up was at 7.30 a.m. and the bus turned up two minutes early. A soldier with a clipboard leapt out of it.

'Morning, lads!' he said. 'You look a cheerful crowd.'

The lads stared back at him, some smiling, some giving it attitude. Scottie nodded in the soldier's direction and waited as one by one they were counted aboard. The scrawny lad with the carrier bag was called Colton.

'Colton from Calton,' said the soldier. 'There's one for you.'

He got on in front of Scottie. Scottie watched him choose a seat away from the others and immediately turn his face to look out of the window.

Scottie stepped on to the bus.

'Mind your head,' said the soldier. 'You might knock some sense into it.'

Scottie and Drew sat three seats back and when the bus pulled away they shot a glance at each other.

'This is it then,' said Drew.

'Aye,' said Scottie. It was all he could say.

Scottie was separated from Drew and billeted in a different place so he hardly caught a glimpse of him. Whenever Scottie was doing one thing, Drew was doing something else. There was too much to take in, no time to rest. He registered, took his medical, stuffed lunch down himself in a big canteen and then spent the afternoon in the gym taking fitness tests. After that it was a room full of computers answering questions. The worst bit was when they had to stand up and tell each other about themselves. Scottie went first and made a right hash of it but it was okay because most of the other lads messed it up too. Lights out was at 11 p.m. and as soon as Scottie's head hit the pillow he felt himself drifting. It didn't matter that there were seven other lads next to him he'd never met because they were off too. All of them were whacked out. The scrawny lad from the bus was in Scottie's billet. He was in the end bed. Scottie could see him in the half-light, lying with his back to the rest of them.

So far he'd done well enough. Even though he had nothing on him he'd managed all of the physical tests with ease. The one that had caused the biggest stir was the 'jerry can' test where they had to carry the two cans to see how far they could get. When the scrawny lad stepped up Scottie watched the instructors to see how they'd react. He watched them as the scrawny lad made his way down the gym, taking things at his own pace, outdistancing Scottie and each of the other lads one at a time until it seemed everybody in the place had stopped what they were doing to watch him. In the end only one other lad got further and he was twice the size and twice the weight. The instructors found the whole thing hilarious and made a point of ribbing the lads about it. Scottie got the impression they were trying to earn the scrawny lad some respect, but they didn't have to bother. He was earning it by himself. Scottie watched the lad lying there as he fell asleep, wondering about him, knowing only what he'd said in the classroom, that he was Colton from Calton, awkwardly repeating the joke, that he'd wanted to join the army since he was ten, that he'd left school a year early, sat around waiting until the day he was old enough to sign up. Slowly, Scottie let the muscles in his body relax, feeling aches and strains in places he'd never known existed, wondering what he was going to feel like in the morning. There was still the run to complete and even though he and Drew had prepared for it, now that it was imminent he wasn't sure they'd prepared for it at all.

6 a.m. next morning. Shouting. Lads rushing about and getting ready for the day. Scottie sighed, thought about forgetting the whole thing, thought about Mel for the shortest second then hoisted himself from his bunk and joined the chaos.

After that it was just like the day before, a few minutes for breakfast, inspection at his bedside, something called a sheet exchange that he had to do against the clock and then out on the tarmac to walk the course he was going to run. The run should have been no big deal but Scottie had problems. It was only a mile and a half and he'd been running more than that with Drew all summer, but his stomach was tight with nerves and he could feel a stitch threatening even before he started. When the whistle blew he knew he had to take it easy, otherwise he was going to make an idiot of himself. Some of the other lads were racing away, eager to be the first. Scottie had expected to do the same but in the last moment he changed his mind. It didn't matter who came first. It wasn't a race against each other. It was a race against himself. He dropped into his own world and pulled focus. It was raining, just like the morning he and Drew had started out on it all. He let the rain fall on his face and enjoyed the feel of it on his skin. Bit by bit his stomach muscles relaxed. That was when he sensed somebody running alongside him, feet striking the tarmac in rhythm just like Drew's had, breathing matching breathing. It was the scrawny lad, Colton from Calton. They ran together, passing lads one at a time, lads that were starting to struggle, lads that had gone off too quickly. Scottie felt a rush of adrenalin, something new and exciting. It wasn't a race, he knew that, but he and the scrawny lad were going to finish first all the same and when they did they each looked at one another and smiled. The instructors were nodding their approval. One by one the other lads trickled in, all of them within the time limit. The last of them spewed his guts up at the finish line but then he broke into a grin when he saw that he'd made it. Scottie watched him and then turned to say something to Colton, but Colton from Calton was way off already, marching towards the billets to get changed, a tiny figure in the huge expanse of the camp.

When they were done with everything the lads were taken to a classroom. They had to wait for their names to be called, and then they were taken to a little office where they'd discover if they were in or out. For Scottie it was the worst part of the whole weekend. He was powerless to do anything about it, had given all he could. Once again he found his mind wandering, inventing scenarios where they told him he wasn't ready, dreading how that might feel, imagining the bus ride home, walking through his mam's front door, everybody waiting for the news, having to break it to them. Each time the office door opened the lads fell silent and each time a name was called a lad got up and disappeared behind the door, leaving the rest to go through the whole thing again and again and again. Eventually, after the longest time, he heard his own name being called. He stood, shot a quick glance at the lads that were still waiting and exited one room to be faced with another, his legs, so sturdy over the whole of the weekend, threatening to collapse under him.

A young officer was sat behind the desk inside the office. He looked Scottie up and down when he entered then went back to checking the pile of papers in front of him. Scottie stood stock still in the middle of the room, desperately trying to hide his nerves.

'I'm not going to mess about,' said the officer. 'You've proved yourself to be all that we're looking for over the last few days. Welcome to the army.'

Scottie didn't hear the rest, just became lost in a blur of words and hand-shaking. He was swelled to bursting and didn't even begin to come down until he was back outside on the tarmac waiting for the coach. It was all there if he wanted it, the next four years laid out on a platter, direction where there had been no direction, money where there had been no money, a life where there had been no life. He felt on top of the world, wanted only to see Mel and break the news.

He was on the coach before Drew appeared.

'You in?' Drew asked.

'Yeah,' said Scottie. 'How about you?'

Drew shook his head.

'No good. It's the asthma. I started wheezing after the run and they picked up on it. They said it can't be trusted. They're going to see what they've got but it won't be for ages.'

'You're joking,' said Scottie. 'How did the run go?'

'Fine. Everything went fine but they're just not happy with the asthma. They said it's too unpredictable and that's that.'

Drew's voice wobbled and he fell silent, gritted his teeth, stared out of the window.

For the rest of the journey the two of them sat quietly next to each other. Scottie could sense Drew boiling and breaking up inside. He knew he was thinking about the janitor job, about seeing it through for another indefinite length of days, weeks, months, even years. He didn't know what to say though, so he said nothing. It was only when they reached the outskirts of the city that Drew spoke again.

'I'm not staying at that school,' he said. 'They're going to have to get me something else because I'm not staying there.'

Scottie looked at him. He thought about his day at the chicken factory and the choices Drew didn't have. He'd known Drew all of his life, had shared so much, had been like a brother to him, but right at that moment he couldn't think how to make things easier. For the first time ever, something was threatening to come between them, something they had no control over. Scottie was in, had his grip on a future. There was no way he was going to let it slip. It was something they were going to have to get used to.

9

Off the bus, he made his way straight to Mel's place, met her at the door and followed behind her up the stairs sporting a glum look on his face, waited until she closed her bedroom door behind them before speaking.

'Piece of cake,' he said.

She looked at him.

'Really?'

He nodded.

'Yeah, really. It was a breeze.'

She stepped up and hugged him, a smile beaming on her face.

'You're pleased then?' he asked.

'Yeah,' she said. 'Of course I am. It's brilliant.'

She manoeuvred around him and then stepped up on to the bed so that she was above him, then she stepped back and saluted him, giggling.

He laughed.

'Pack it in,' he said.

But she didn't pack it in.

Instead she said, 'Get down and give me twenty, soldier!'

'No way!'

'Go on. Show me what you're made of.'

He shook his head but somehow he still found himself dropping to his knees on her bedroom carpet, kneeling forward, placing his hands on the floor.

'This is stupid,' he said.

'Just do it,' she said. 'It's an order.'

He started doing press-ups but she stopped him.

'Take your top off,' she said. 'I want to see those muscles flexing.'

'What?'

But he didn't have a chance to refuse. She was at him, pawing and pulling his top over his head.

'That's better,' she said. 'Now get on with it.'

He started off again, doing them the way they'd said, Mel counting each time his nose touched the carpet. Because he was doing them properly it started hurting at twenty but Mel told him to keep going and he wanted to show her he could do it so he carried on, focusing on the carpet below him and then closing his eyes to fight the pain. He got to thirty-five before he collapsed in a heap and rolled over on to his back. Above him, Mel had stripped to her underwear.

'What are you doing?' he grinned.

'Nothing,' she said but she started jumping up and down on the bed as she said it, acting like a five-year-old.

'What if your mam comes in?'

'She won't,' she said. 'She's at Mass.'

'Really?'

'Really.'

'I think I'll spend a few more weekends away,' he said and he couldn't stop himself from grinning again, thinking about the army, thinking about the future, staring at Mel in her Little Miss Naughty underwear in the bedroom with the Bible and the rosary.

10

He was waiting for Drew to come out of work when old Saunders appeared at the gate.

'I thought you couldn't wait to leave us,' Saunders said.

'I'm waiting for Drew,' said Scottie.

'He's another one. What's he doing in that job?'

'It's all he could get.'

Saunders gave a look that said he didn't really believe it.

'How about you?' he asked. 'What are you up to?'

'Had my army selection last weekend,' said Scottie.

Saunders stiffened.

'And?'

'I got in. Training starts next month. Six months from now I'll be in for real.'

It looked like Saunders was going to say something but just then Drew turned up.

'Here he is,' said Saunders. 'Janitor extraordinaire.'

Drew laughed.

'Bet you couldn't believe it when you saw me,' said Drew.

'You could say that again,' said Saunders. 'Anyway, good to see you, Scottie lad. Good to see you looking well.'

'Nae dramas,' said Scottie.

They left Saunders at the gate and started down the road into town.

'Want a quick game at The Thistle?' Scottie asked.

'Aye,' said Drew. 'Best of three if you like. I need to whip you a few more times before you're off.'

'Some chance,' said Scottie. He looked back over his shoulder. Saunders was still there, watching them.

'He's all right is old Saunders,' said Scottie.

'Yeah?' said Drew. 'Well, I can tell you one or two stories about him. Jimmy tells me everything.'

'Really?'

'Really. Remember that maths teacher who started when we were in year ten, the one that only stayed about six months?'

'The blondie?'

'Aye.'

'How can I forget?'

Drew pointed over his shoulders towards where Saunders was still standing and winked.

'You're kidding,' said Scottie. 'She was half his age!'

'His wife found out.'

'Really?'

'Aye. That's why he's standing there. He's waiting for his wife to collect him. She doesn't give him any rope these days.'

'Old Saunders. You're sure Jimmy's not just having you on?'

'Straight up, mate. He's a real dark horse.'

As they turned the corner Scottie took one last glance behind him. Saunders was still there, a small figure against the railings. Scottie remembered the day they started at the school, how Saunders was the most terrifying teacher they came across. Now he gave him a wave. Saunders waved back. He still had his arm up when they turned the corner and he still looked like he had something on his mind, something he wanted to say to Scottie that needed to be said, something to get off his chest, something serious he was struggling to attach his voice to.

Thin threads of light appeared on the horizon, hardly registering to begin with, just brushing against the dark above, but as Scottie watched from the window the light gathered. The great grey city remained silent, its rooftops still covered in crusty snow, its people hunkered down and wrapped up warm against the cold. There was no place in all of this for a lost boy. The city had nothing to offer.

Scottie's chest and shoulder ached, the same dull ache as before. It wasn't getting any better. If anything it was growing worse. He winced each time he tried to alter the way he was sitting. He was thirsty, too. An hour or so before he'd tried to find water, had wandered the old familiar corridors searching for the toilets but when he got to them he found them locked. He tried the science rooms next, remembering the days when he'd rush to the sink at the back to wash acid from his skin after they'd messed around with it, Mackie laughing and not bothering, coming to school the next day with sores and burns. The water in the science rooms was turned off, too. He thought about Drew with his list of jobs to complete before the holiday and he shook his head. He'd not thought things through properly and was angry at himself. He was tired, that was the problem. He couldn't remember the last time he'd slept. Now he was nervous to do so, frightened they'd come while he was out of it, catch him by surprise, not give him a chance to show them what he was all about.

But he had to sleep, if only for a short while. It was drawing him in and it was better to go prepared than to fight it and not be ready.

He crawled to the classroom door, keeping low, pushed it open and peered into the corridor. There was a set of double doors at either end. He'd dealt with them both, piled up barricades of desks and chairs. Now he did the same to the classroom door, dragged desks and chairs across the flooring, the shuddering sound echoing through the building, sounding much louder than it surely was. The same would happen if they came. He'd hear them and would have time to ready himself. He *didn't need long, just the time it took to pick up his rifle, get what he had to say off his chest. After that . . . well, it didn't matter what happened after that.*

When Scottie was done with the stacking he went back to the window, light spreading across the landscape now, the hardened snow glistening beneath it. He rested below the window with his back to the wall. He knew this place, old Saunders' room, had spent five long years of his life here. He could picture himself sat at the back with Mackie, paying no attention, having no pen, no bag, nothing with him, just the torn scruffed-up exercise book that Saunders kept for him on the desk, nothing in it except a few dates and half-written titles. In the end Saunders had been happy enough just to have the ones in the back row in their seats, had concentrated all his energy on the ones at the front who gave a toss. Scottie crawled over to the little office where Saunders kept his computer. There wasn't much in there, just a desk, piles of textbooks, a revolving chair that had seen better days. How many times had Scottie been sent to sit in that chair on his own? How many times had he sat there with his hands underneath his thighs, spinning the chair with his feet, killing time, waiting for the lesson to end? Scottie spotted something on the wall above the computer screen, photos of the football teams Saunders had run, the years counting back one by one, the photos fading. There was Scottie's team, just two pictures in, and there were Scottie and Drew standing at the back, arms folded, staring out of the frame, smiling mischievously, not realising what they were heading towards.

It didn't matter though. None of it mattered. It had all led up to this moment, and even if he had known that this was his future he'd have been powerless to do anything about it. There had been nothing when school finished, just a void to suffocate in and then the army had taken him and given him a chance to breathe and that chance had led to this. Mel had given him a chance to prove himself and that chance had led to this. Everything had led to this.

Back to the wall, running the chain of his St Christopher necklace between his fingers, the classroom set out as it always had been save for the desks and chairs he'd piled, Scottie's mind drifted to the other classroom in the other place. He could hear the whizz and pop of gun-fire, could see blood on the walls and floor, blood on his clothing too, feel a dull, empty ache spreading through his body, causing the light and life of the moment to fracture and let the first shreds of darkness in.

11

He was walking Mel home from work on the same Friday, walking up Hillside towards her place, sharing a bag of chips, when she stopped and sat on the benches outside the cemetery. It was early closing for the hairdresser's and the two of them were supposed to be getting ready for a big night on the town. Except she didn't seem up for it, had been quiet since he'd walked into the salon, had hardly spoken to him while he joked with Maureen at the counter, or when they'd stopped for the chips, the usual Friday ritual.

'What is it?' he asked.

For a while she didn't respond, just sat on her hands on the bench while he stood over her munching away. Then she said,

'Have you thought about it?'

'About what?'

'You know what,' she said.

He shrugged his shoulders.

'The army,' she said. 'Have you thought about it? Where they might send you? Where you might end up? What might happen to you?'

He turned himself sideways and sat on the bench.

'Not really,' he said. 'There's not much point because you never know. That's what makes it special.'

'You know where they might send you though,' she said. 'You know it's not like it used to be.'

'How do you mean?'

'Not a soft option any more.'

'I don't think the army's ever been a soft option,' he said.

'I know. But it used to be easier than it is now.'

'The older blokes at the camp kept saying it's easier now. You know, not like it was in their day . . .'

But he knew exactly what she was talking about, was simply trying to deflect her argument. He stood up again, walked to the bin by the cemetery gates and chucked the chip bag in.

'I thought you were all for it,' he said.

'I was. I am. But think about it. You could get something here. Something that didn't mean you had to be off every five minutes.'

'When I was looking you were always at me,' he said.

'That's because you weren't looking. Not really.'

'Because nothing did it for me,' he said. 'It was all the same rubbish. This is different.'

When she didn't say anything he sat down next to her again. After a minute she moved so he could put his arm across her shoulders and pull her close to him.

'I'm just scared,' she said.

'Scared of what?'

She shook her head, remained silent.

'Don't be,' he said. 'Think of the money instead.'

'It'll be nice to see you with some of your own,' she said.

'Exactly,' he said.

'Then you can get Friday chips every once in a while.'

'No chance,' he said. 'That's your job. It's tradition.'

12

His training started in March, fourteen weeks to begin with and then fourteen weeks more if it all went to plan. It started slowly, the lads sitting through lecture after boring lecture, fighting their instincts to act up like most of them would have at school, Scottie sitting on his hands whenever he wasn't writing something down so that he didn't fall into his old ways. It was a real battle. When they weren't in lectures they were out on the square doing drill. Some of the lads started bitching about it, whining that they should have gone to college, whining that it wasn't what they'd signed up for. The only sign of what was to come was the kit they were issued. There was too much of it and some of them couldn't cope. They started taking short cuts when it came to keeping the place tidy, started not bothering with cleaning up after themselves. Bit by bit the barracks became a mess.

Scottie fought the boredom of it all by eating, stuffing himself in between meals. It became a joke and the lads were always on about it.

'Hey, Scottie, how many burgers have you squeezed into your Bergen?'

'What's for second breakfast?'

Stuff like that, every day.

But things changed. It happened one morning about two

weeks in. The army came at them full on and sent some of
them reeling. The lads were forced to get the barracks spotless
and the ones that had let things get out of hand were hit the
hardest. Scottie was glad of it. He'd kept his bit in order the
best he could and he was sick of walking through other
people's rubbish. But he didn't get away clean. The corporals
used him as an example to the others and forced him to take
on the role of ensuring all the lads were up to scratch. They
were given crap jobs to do like cleaning the toilets and when
they weren't done properly Scottie was the one that got it in
the neck.

In the evenings he called Mel, always last thing before
lights out. Sometimes they were on the phone for an hour,
talking about everything and nothing. He regretted it the
mornings after, for losing sleep he couldn't afford to lose, then
the next evening he'd do exactly the same. He spoke to his
mam on Sundays, caught up on the week's events. She was
always upset at the end of the call so once a week was enough
for both of them.

By the fourth week some of the lads were flagging. One or
two gave it up and went home. The rest got through it by
taking the piss out of each other in the evenings, searching out
some characteristic to home in on. Scottie lapped it up. All of
the years with Drew and Mackie were coming in handy now.
All the lads had something, some chink in their armour. He'd
come out of it all right with his eating. They picked up on
Colton for his scrawny legs and McDonald for his hairy back.
One day after he'd messed up on the assault course the lads
pinned McDonald down and waxed his back for him using an
old roll of insulating tape. It was a laugh. McDonald's back
was red raw for two days but he took it on the chin. Everybody had some sort of prank to face. Scottie waited for his,
then one day one of the lads came in with three massive packs
of takeaway hamburgers. They sat him in a chair and placed

bets on how many he could eat. He got through seven, munching away until the lads were all sat with their bottom jaws on the floor.

'He's like a machine.'

'Where does he put it all?'

Just after Scottie had stuffed the seventh burger into his mouth the sergeant came in and told them they were going on a tab. He said they had ten minutes to get ready. That was the joke. The lads had known about it and kept it a secret. They had another round of bets on how far Scottie would go before throwing up, counting the distance in sections of a mile. Scottie did the whole run without being sick, without even breaking stride, while the other lads trailed in behind him.

'It's all about stocking up with fuel,' he laughed. 'You lot should try it.'

After that they called him 'burger man' and the name stuck right through the fourteen weeks until even the sergeant was calling him by that name. The training took Scottie back to his childhood and, revelling in it, he got himself an identity. That was the thing that sealed it.

13

Friday night. The lads headed off into town on a binge.
Scottie went with them. There was nothing else to do except
stay on the camp and watch DVDs. He called Mel and gave
her an update and then joined the others. Only Colton didn't
come. He said he had things to do, letters to write, stuff like
that. The lads tried to persuade him but he was having none of
it. In the end they chucked on their bests and left him to it.
They got some looks from the locals just walking down the
road, eight raw squaddies ready for a night on the tiles, tempt-
ing pickings for any lads who thought they might be hard
enough.

It was 7 p.m. when they left and by nine most of the group
were pissed off their faces. Scottie paced himself. He wasn't
into it. What he wanted was to get away for the weekend, to
see Mel and spend the night in the shed with her, to wake up
with her, to catch up with Drew and Mackie and tell them
what he'd been up to, find out what they were doing, talk
about the Hoops, set the world to rights. Instead he was stuck
watching the lads force pint after pint down like there was no
tomorrow, all the while two different sets of eyes watching
them, the local girls who were happy to cop off with a squaddie every now and then just for the craic and the local lads
who hated them for being different and thinking they were
special, the lads with chips on their shoulders about strangers,

the lads with some point to prove. Things were bound to kick off eventually.

After midnight, with things tightening up inside the club, Scottie slipped outside and wandered over to the burger bar, fishing in his pocket for change. It was partly because he was famished and partly because he just wanted out of the place. There was a girl working on the counter and he got talking to her, told her where he was from and what had brought him there. It was the first girl he'd talked to in weeks. She was brunette, pretty, and she had a glint in her eye. He wondered what she was doing working in a burger stall, thought about asking, but it was him doing all the talking really, not her. He told her about how being out with the army boys was differ-ent from drinking with Drew and Mackie. He knew how those two clicked, he said. The three of them could argue the toss and be at each other's throats for twenty minutes then sink into silence and not speak for the next twenty but they'd still be mates and at the end of it all they went home to their beds. He told her how he hardly knew these lads, how they laughed and joked and took the piss just the same but how there was always the chance one of them might turn. None of them knew how to be quiet around the others either and somebody was always going too far, nerves forever straining to breaking point.

They had all this aggression building inside of them and nowhere to release it. It was being forced into them on a daily basis and some of the lads couldn't control it so it all came out after a few beers. On this night it started with glances, words exchanged with some lad who had his pint knocked from his grip and then they were at it, fists and boots flying, heads, knees, elbows, the works, a right mess. Eventually, it spilled out on to the kerb.

Scottie watched the whole thing unfold from the safety of the burger van. He was caught in two minds. One said dive in and the other said get away before the military police got wind of it. The lads were looking at trouble if they were caught. He stuffed one burger into his mouth and the second one in his jacket pocket and sloped away, the girl smiling at him one last time. He got himself off the main drag and back to the barracks as quickly as he could, knowing that the more distance and time he could put between himself and the fight the better. He had a plan. He'd tell the lads he'd left before the trouble started. It was sort of true because he'd been chatting to the girl in the van for a good ten minutes and when he'd left the lads to go outside there hadn't been any trouble. He'd play the innocent and give them his big gentle smile and they'd believe him for sure.

He didn't get away with it, though. In the days that followed they were put through it, the whole lot of them. Tabs were tougher, cleaning duties longer, drill sessions never-ending. Even Colton got it. When he tried to tell the sergeant that he'd not even gone out the sergeant called him a soft bastard for not taking the opportunity to chase a bird, for not being there in the thick of it when it kicked off. So there was no escaping the fallout, no being different, no opportunity to be anything else but part of the whole.

14

The thing he was best at was anything to do with his rifle, his SA80. It was his weapon, his lifeline. He connected with it the moment they issued it to him. He was the fastest when it came to stripping it down for cleaning, the most precise when it came to caring for its parts, the most precious of it and the most accurate with it on the range. It came naturally to him, like he'd been doing it all his life. It wasn't long before the instructors had him helping others and it wasn't long before the others came to him with questions about what they were doing wrong.

Colton had a lot of problems with it, especially on the range when they were firing live ammunition.

'You need to work on your shoulders,' said Scottie. 'You need to build yourself up. There's too much bone there and not enough muscle.'

Colton did as Scottie told him and bit by bit he got better at it.

Scottie was on top of the world whenever they were doing anything with their SA80s, the first one on the range, the first one to call out answers in lectures. In the end the instructors told him not to say anything so the others could have a chance to show what they knew. He sailed through the weapons test. At night in the billets lads would come to him looking for tips and pointers, how to get a round off accurately, how to stay concentrated on the target, how to get through the test like he had. There was no explaining it for most of them though. It was just something he could do and they couldn't. There was no magic formula. And there were things he struggled with just like they did. Drill was his real hate. He couldn't get it right. As the weeks ticked by the one thing that worried him at night was the passing-out parade. He dreaded making a tosser of himself in front of the top brass. Mel would be there. His mam and uncle would be there too.

It was his uncle that finally got him sorted. One Sunday night he grabbed the phone from Scottie's mam. He was slurring his words, the worse for drink, but told Scottie not to think about it, told him it was all a load of crap, told him he could still be a brilliant soldier without mastering how to march up and down a square. It worked. When Scottie stopped thinking about it he got better, so that's what he told the other lads when they came to him with their problems on the range.

'Try not to think about it,' he said. 'Just let it come . . .'

The lads sloped off and looked at him like he was no help at all, but one by one they got through the test and one by one they came up to him in their own ways to tell him thanks. Colton was the most grateful. He only passed the test with a week to spare.

15

On the coldest, wettest April Saturday imaginable the lads
held an eighteenth birthday bash for Scottie by forcing him
into a minibus for a day of paintball. It was playing at war but
there was a competitive edge to it. Guys were there with clipboards, scoring points.

'Let's see if you squaddies are really as tough as you make
out,' said one.

In the first game Scottie's team had to defend their base
from an all-out attack. Scottie took up a position behind an
old four-tonner, got himself low down by the back wheel and
waited for the whistle to blow. When it did, all hell broke
loose. Within seconds bullets were whizzing over his head,
splattering against the trees behind him. All he could do was
make himself small, curl up tight. He couldn't fire his weapon,
couldn't get in position to do it without exposing himself.
Bullets rained in against the metal plating on the side of the
truck, ping, ping, pinging, much louder than he'd expected.
All he could do was think about how much one of them
might hurt if it hit him. For a week the lads had been telling
stories about it, about the welts and bruises they'd picked up
doing it until Scottie was sure it was bound to hurt because
they liked it to be that way. He was a little kid here, a traitor
to his size, scrunched up, useless, doing nothing except waiting for the whistle to blow and the game to be over.

When the first scenario ended the lads grouped together and shared their stories. Most of them had paint on them, either splatters where the bullets had exploded near them or great splodges where they'd been hit clean and 'killed'. Scottie was spotless from head to toe.

'Hey, burger man,' shouted McDonald. 'Have you been and got changed already?'

Scottie laughed to hide it.

'It's called skill, mate,' he said.

Atkinson was the only other one with a pellet-free uniform but his was covered in mud and leaves instead. There wasn't a dry part to be seen. He stood there amongst them, impassive. He'd been right in the thick of it for sure and he'd come out untouched. He was like some super-hero, immune to danger. He talked about how many kills he'd made and nobody argued with him.

The lads compared how many pellets they'd fired, talked in fifties and hundreds. Scottie kept his mouth shut. He'd hardly fired any, just randomly stuck his gun above the parapet for a second and squeezed off a couple of shots at nothing, not even looking to see what he was firing at. The scorers checked them over again, made notes and wrote on their clipboards.

One of them whispered in Scottie's ear.

'The bullets aren't rationed, mate. They might cost a few quid but surely the army doesn't pay that badly.'

The teams changed objectives, the attackers becoming defenders and the defenders becoming attackers.

Scottie crept through the undergrowth, moving silently. He could see the enemy base ahead. They were in there, guarding the place like he had, waiting. Every now and then one of the lads in his team fired off a round. There was the tiny crack as they pulled the trigger and the ping of the pellet hitting the metal barricades. The shots were wasted though. The lads just couldn't resist firing them off. Scottie crawled flat on his belly, the undergrowth soaking him, soggy wet leaves sticking to him, branches and twigs scratching his skin and pulling at his clothing. When he got his head up he could see the base more clearly but he couldn't make out any of the lads inside. Triggers were cracking more regularly now as things started heating up. Scottie got himself behind a tree and nestled down just in time. One, two, three pellets whacked into the bark above his head. He spread himself on the ground behind the tree, keeping his head down. He heard one of the other lads race past him, drawing fire. From the corner of his eye Scottie watched as the lad threw himself to the ground, paintballs breaking up in the branches in front of him, all the colours of the rainbow.

Scottie felt useless. He had to do something. What good was he to anybody lying here on the ground while the lads carried on the battle without him? He dragged himself to his knees and poked his head above the V shape of the tree stump. Whack! A pellet hit him clean between the eyes, exploded against his goggles, blinding him. Then another pellet hit and another, one hitting him on his chin, right on the bone. He turned around, a fourth pellet striking him on the back of his head. He shouted,

'All right, all right! Jesus Christ!'

The observer pointed through the woods, ordering him to leave the battle, which he did, cleaning his goggles as he went.

That was it, then. That was game over. Trudging up the slope between the trees to where the other 'dead' lads were huddled in the drizzle, the crack and whizz of the battle becoming lost somewhere in the trees, he had time to think about it. What if it had been for real? What if it was a real bullet? What would a bullet do to a person if it hit them clean on the forehead like that?

Then he stopped himself thinking about it because thinking about something like that for more than a second could send a soldier mad and he was going to be a soldier one day, not some dropout.

The day went on and on and all through the day it rained, rain on the verge of sleet, rain that froze Scottie's fingers and his face, sent chills running to the very heart of his being. By early afternoon it stopped being serious, the lads not caring who got shot and who didn't. They started launching kamikaze attacks into their opponents bases, taking it in turns, getting shot to pieces and then coming back to compare bruises, doing anything and everything to keep their minds from the miserable weather. Scottie tried to keep his head down, hoping each time a phase ended that they were going to call it a day. Just when he thought it might be over, McDonald came over with a grin on his face.

'Hey, big man,' he said. 'It's time you were sent on a mission.'

Pretty soon Scottie was in the middle of the enemy camp, pellets fizzing past his ears, pellets smacking against his arms and legs, pellets whacking against his body in a non-stop wave. He was almost through it when a shout came up from behind him. He turned to see McDonald leading the lads from his own team against him. They got within a few metres and then they let him have it with everything they had left. He ended up curled up in a ball on the sodden ground, covered in paint from head to toe.

When it was over the lads pulled him to his feet and sang him a birthday tune.

'Serves you right for being such a miserable bastard,' laughed McDonald as they drove back to camp. Scottie smiled and pretended he found the whole thing hilarious but the truth was he didn't find it funny at all. He loved the army already but sometimes he hated having to be an army lad and he wondered if that part of him would always be missing.

The next weekend, his real birthday weekend, he went home. They had a celebration in The Thistle: Drew, Mackie, Mel, his mam and sis, the whole lot of them there. His Uncle Jack wasn't up to much. Mel came back to the hut after to stay the night. Lying on their sofa, the two of them talked about the future.

'I've four weeks,' he said. 'Then that's it over with.'

'You mean then it's just starting,' said Mel. 'What's the word on your posting?'

'There's no word,' he said. 'Nobody knows anything about it.'

'What if they post you miles away?'

'They won't.'

He stopped talking after that. He was lying but he didn't want the conversation going where the lads always took it on camp. They talked around and around it and always ended up back in the same place. It was hardly surprising because it was on the news every day. None of them wanted to end up there but most of them had a feeling that was exactly where they were going. Rumours spread around the place on a daily basis, lads hearing this and that, imagining things, getting things mixed up, but no matter how much they tried to stop them happening the rumours wouldn't go away.

He woke to the sound of footsteps. They were in the corridor, moving quietly, moving towards the classroom. He grabbed the rifle and shuffled across the floor, pressed himself against the opposite wall so that if the door burst open he would be behind it. It would give him a fighting chance. He wasn't there two seconds when the footsteps stopped. There was a moment of waiting in which he felt his senses stirring, his fingers gripping the rifle tightly, his breathing shallow, eyes fixed on the door handle, waiting for the slightest movement.

No movement came though. Instead, the footsteps started up again, moved away along the corridor, disappeared from his hearing.

For a long time he waited, expecting the footsteps to return. His head started to fill with questions. One set of footsteps made no sense. It wasn't how things were done. It should have been clean, room to room, a dozen men at least, swift and brutal. He shuffled back across the room to the window and peeked out, expecting to see a change now but there was no change except for the light of day. A flock of pigeons swooped over the school and dived in the direction of the church. A tabby cat stepped tentatively across the playground, conspicuous against the whiteness of the snow. A gritter made its way slowly up Hillside, its engine droning and yellow lights flashing. There was no other traffic. It was Sunday morning, still early and everything was the way it had always been on a Sunday morning, the city waking slowly from slumber, the snow cushioning every sound. He was irrelevant amongst it all.

But the footsteps had been real, there was no questioning that. He tried to make sense of them. The caretaker? He would have reacted to the stacked chairs and desks in the corridor. He'd have come into the room to see, surely. An intruder then, someone like him, a homeless geezer who'd found the smashed window and come to get out of the cold, come to see what he could find.

Maybe.

Perhaps.

Probably.

He couldn't come up with anything better.

16

Deepest May. Mountain country. Final exercise. It should have been the beginning of summer but instead it rained and rained, rolling black masses of cloud converging on the moorland, dark shadows on the hills. Scottie and the lads struggled beneath it all, tiny and pathetic in the vast landscape. It was the last challenge, the last thing separating them from what they were striving towards. There was nothing to do but grit their teeth and get on with it. Trudging through mud, the rain falling in icy sheets, Scottie searched inside himself for the will to go on. He was beginning to have doubts. He'd never felt so miserable, so exhausted, so out of it. They'd tabbed for miles in full kit, their boots sinking, the mud sticking, each step a trial. And there had been no let-up in the rain that fell, soaking their uniforms, chilling them to the bone. All this to prove they were worthy of the name of the regiment, all this to prove they had what it took.

Setting up their harbour area on the first night was almost beyond them. They reached the spot later than expected. It was dark already. The ground was saturated. They were freezing cold, their fingers unwilling to cooperate. In blinking red torchlight they did their best to make shelter. The night was a battle of will, the rain not letting up for a moment, their rations barely edible, the lads struggling to get shut-eye in between standing guard.

On the second morning, the rain still falling, they planned their attack on the enemy position. Atkinson took charge. They tabbed until the terrain matched their maps and then they went to ground, waiting for the order.

Crouched deep in heather, separated from the lads due to the spacing, Scottie fought to keep himself focused and awake. All he wanted to do was to go back to camp, get out of his clothes, get a shower and crash. He'd had it with the whole experience. It was too much to ask of somebody. In his head he imagined squaring up to the officers on the base, flooring one when they stepped into his reach. But they'd done it, all of them. That was the great leveller. You couldn't knock somebody who'd done it before you. When they were through with it, when it was over, he'd be one of those in the know. He'd have the credentials to grin and make comments to others. It was how the army worked, experience layered on experience, the cream rising to the top.

And so he waited in the heather, waited for the signal to move, for an hour and then another. No signal came. He guessed this was all part of the test, to see which of them would crack at the final hurdle, to see which one of them would break cover and give the game away, so he kept low and huddled deeper into himself, thinking of Mel and downing a pint with Drew in The Thistle, the fire burning there, the heat of it warming him through to the guts.

The rain turned to a fine drizzle and mist dropped over the heather. There were twenty other lads like him crouched in the place but with the mist and the silence it was too easy for him to believe he was the only one there. He became disorientated. He wasn't sure which way was forwards and when the shout came up to move he hesitated for as long as it took to see the direction the lads either side of him were running. He caught the slightest sight of them through the mist, hunched figures dashing away and he went after them. Soon he was running on open moorland, against the gradient, legs pumping, boots splashing through soggy ground, sometimes slipping, always moving forwards. Some of the lads started firing, the sound of each shot dispersing into the mist. He reached some craggy boulders, dropped beside them, fired off a couple of rounds in the direction of the tor where the enemy were, then scurried forward again, keeping his head down, moving and firing, keeping up with the others, doing as they did, doing what he'd been trained to do the best he could.

Afterwards, enemy defeated, the lads sat amongst the boulders and rocks of the tor taking a breather. It would have been good to think the exercise was at an end but they were only halfway through it. There was another day and night to go, two more attacks to plan and carry out, thirty hours or more left to endure. Atkinson was busy as usual, buoying up the troops with slaps on the back and applause. He was good at it. Scottie could see the officer in him sprouting out of his uniform. The lads respected him and this exercise was only going to cement that feeling. From the beginning, while others had waned, Scottie included, Atkinson had been driving them on, sometimes with jokes to make light of the situation, sometimes with motivational chit-chat, sometimes with shouts and kicks up the arse. It all worked, which was why he was doing it now, but something seemed to be troubling him. He was stood amongst the group, checking faces.

'What is it?' Scottie asked him.

'Maybe nothing,' he said. Then he said, 'Have you seen Miller?'

Scottie looked about him. The lads were spread about the rocks on the tor. He couldn't see Miller anywhere.

'Has he gone for a piss?' Scottie asked.

'If he has, he's taking his time,' said Atkinson.

'Do you think they took him prisoner?'

Atkinson shook his head.

'They wouldn't do that,' he said. 'Besides, they didn't have a chance. We'd have seen.'

Scottie knew he was right. All the enemy had been 'killed'. They'd since departed in their truck, set off back to camp to dry out and warm up. Later tonight they'd be at the second coordinate, defending it in darkness, a different enemy with the same face. If they'd made a mess of the attack, if they'd offered a route for escape, then maybe Miller could have been taken, but there had been no such opportunity. The attack had gone like clockwork. The tor had been surrounded and then they'd closed in on its defenders. To effect.

'What do you reckon then?' Scottie asked.

Atkinson shook his head. Scottie turned and looked back over the ground they'd covered, or the little of it he could see before the mist engulfed it.

'We'd best learn when we lost him,' said Atkinson.

The lads grouped together on the tor. They all remembered Miller being with them when they gathered for the assault at the foot of the mountain but nobody had seen him since they'd gone to ground in the heather. The lads flanking him had been too busy with what they were doing to notice.

'And you couldn't tell who was who anyway,' said one of them. 'Not in the mist. I could hardly make out who was on our side and who wasn't.'

Scottie nodded his head. It was true. They'd been firing blanks on the exercise. God only knew how they'd have managed it with live rounds. It was so easy to aim a rifle at one of your own, so easy to . . .

He shut off the thought. What mattered was finding Miller.

'We're gonna have to go back,' he said.

'Have we got time?' Atkinson asked.

'Who cares?' said Scottie. 'We can't leave him. What if he's hurt?'

'What would we do if this was for real? We've a job to do.'

'Yeah, but it isn't real,' said Scottie. 'It's just an exercise. If they throw that one at us we'll just have to do it all again. If we're lucky it might not be raining.'

'It always rains,' said one lad. 'They wait until it forecasts rain before they throw you out in it.'

'We go back then,' said Scottie. 'If we fan out we'll find him.'

So that's what they did, spread themselves out in a line around the tor and started down the hill through the heather, searching for Miller, shouting his name in the mist. They did that for an hour, Scottie and Atkinson coordinating the whole thing, the two of them falling on responsibility like it was the most natural thing in the world, the rest of the lads happy that somebody was taking charge, egos no longer a factor, each and every one of them searching for their lost mate.

But they didn't find him. When they reached the tree line Scottie decided to call things to a halt. They'd never find him in the trees and besides, he'd been with them when they came out of the forest.

'He has to be up there,' he said. 'We must have missed him.'

'We were screaming our heads off,' said one of the lads. 'How could that happen?'

'Maybe he's unconscious,' said Scottie.

'How could he be unconscious?' said the lad.

'I don't know,' said Scottie. 'But it's the only thing I can think of.'

'I'm going to radio in,' said Atkinson. 'This is above our heads.'

The lads agreed. They'd given it their best. Scottie was having none of it though.

'You can radio in,' he said. 'But we need to keep looking until they get here.'

This time they did it differently, sectoring off an area, walking closer together, scanning the heather beneath their feet, not looking anywhere else, listening for a sound and listening too for the buzz of helicopters.

'They'll not see anything in this mist,' said Atkinson. 'I doubt they'll even send a helicopter up.'

'It's up to us then,' Scottie said. He was getting desperate, thinking about Miller lying in the heather, maybe with his head in a puddle, drowned even.

They found him twenty minutes later, just as two officers turned up to see what the trouble was. The lad that discovered him actually tripped over his boots. He was curled up in a ball in the heather, sleeping like a baby. The officers took him back to camp and told the rest of the lads to get on with the exercise and make up the time. When they finished the exercise the next day, Miller's bed at the billet was empty and his stuff was gone. He was 'back squadded' for falling asleep on duty and would have to go through the whole of the last three months of training again. Then, at the end of it, he'd have to do the same exercise. Scottie was gutted for him but Atkinson didn't have any sympathy.

'If he does that in the field somebody might get killed,' he said. 'What if he was on stag?'

'He was just knackered,' said Scottie. 'It could happen to any of us.'

'Yeah, it could happen,' said Atkinson. 'But it doesn't. That's the difference.'

17

Spruced up in his bests on the parade ground, warm in the sunlight, Scottie stood waiting for his name to be called, waiting for the moment when he officially became a soldier. The regimental flags were flying, the band playing, everything spick and span. Scottie could see his own face in the shine of his boots, feel the glints of light reflecting off every polishable surface on the camp. His mam, sis, Mel and Uncle Jack were there; Mel in a red dress, her hair done up, more beautiful than ever, but his uncle looking so sick that Scottie almost didn't recognise him. His mam started crying and even his sister looked like she might lose it. For one day at least though, they left all of the other stuff out of it, not once mentioning the worries he knew they had. His uncle threw him a wink and nodded and Scottie was pretty certain he knew what the wink was for, pretty certain his uncle had been busy repairing damage before it happened. He had a knack for that sort of thing.

Scottie had his photo taken with the lot of them. He wasn't one for photos but on this day he didn't mind. He was as fit as he'd ever been, stronger than he'd ever been, more alert to the things around him, photos were a breeze.

McDonald came over. When he spotted Mel his jaw dropped to the floor.

'Hey, burger man, is that your missus?' he asked. 'I wouldn't mind . . .'

'In your dreams,' Scottie said to him.

'She'll be in my dreams all right,' said McDonald. 'You don't have to worry about that.'

It was a perfect day and when it was over nobody could say he hadn't achieved anything in his life any more because he had. He grabbed Mel and pulled her close.

'What have you to say to me?' he asked her.

She kissed him once, twice, three times and then grinned the way she always did when she was about to bring him down a peg.

'Where are you taking me tonight?'

He picked her up, threw her over his shoulder and carried her away from the crowd. She screamed and screamed. He span her around until she was begging him to stop and then he set her down. She was dizzy and had to hold on to him to stop herself falling.

'Wherever you want to go,' he said. He meant it too. He couldn't have meant it more if he'd said it another thousand times.

18

'**Parade in** five minutes!'

Scottie was in the shower on camp when they called him and he still had soap in his hair when he took his place on the parade ground. He pulled himself to attention when ordered and tried to ignore the itch that was spreading across his neck and shoulders. Something was happening. It was as clear as day to see that. The officers were going about things differently, talking about something, checking clipboards and pacing up and down. A murmur started to spread amongst the lads.

'This is it,' said one.

'Told you,' said another.

'Nah, it'll be a load of crap,' said McDonald. 'It always is.'

But it wasn't a load of crap. A senior officer appeared and came straight out with it, told them they were going to the place they'd all been hearing and talking about. He told them they'd be going in three weeks and that they'd get the details soon enough, told them to go and let it sink in for a while, let their hair down and do whatever they had to do. Walking back to the quarters, Scottie watched the faces of the lads he'd trained with and the lads he'd never seen before. They all wore the same wide-mouthed expressions. In the hours that followed none of them knew what to do with themselves. They paced around the barracks, made phone calls, got together and talked, with no real clue what they were on about, each one taking the lead from another. When the news came on the TV they all watched it to see what was happening out there but nothing was happening on this night so it was back to pacing and talking again until in the end they all went to the bar together and sank as many pints as they could stomach. They were torn, that was the truth of it, torn between the need for travel, adventure, excitement, the chance to do their job for real, the danger that might come with it and the easy life at home, the things they were going to leave behind, the things they imagined they were about to go through and the things they could never have imagined in a lifetime.

In the end he had to check the footsteps out. He moved the chairs one at a time, not making a sound. The desks were more difficult but he did a good job on them, lifting them steadily despite the pain in his shoulder, moving them just enough. Finally he fastened his grip on the door handle and slowly turned it.

The corridor was empty, the chairs and desks undisturbed, still stacked as he'd left them, still doing their job. Scottie checked out the two classrooms to his left. They were empty too. He turned and made his way across the corridor to the room opposite, knowing that the intruder had to be in there, his finger on the trigger of his rifle, his knuckles white with tension.

The classroom was empty, chairs stacked on desks, echoes of the last day of term hanging in the air, the whole place absent of life. Scottie moved silently back to the geography room, his mind doing cartwheels, trying to make sense of the moment, struggling to remain in it, wondering if he was dreaming.

She was stood in the corner of the room when he entered. She had dark eyes. When he looked into them she smiled.

'You?' he said. 'What are you doing here?'

Part Two

19

Scottie's mam discovered his Uncle Jack collapsed in the bathroom at his place less than a month after Scottie became a soldier, his disease, like all of the other things, finally getting the better of him. Uncle Jack died a week later. Scottie was at the hospital when it happened, there with his mam and sis. When he stepped out of the ward afterwards, the first thing he thought of was the shed, of being in there with Little Mackie and Drew, of splitting open a tinnie and getting stuck into the football, so that pretty soon nothing in the world would matter apart from how the Hoops were playing. At half-time Mackie'd shoot down to the chippie and be back for the whistle with three bags of McFadden's finest. The shed would be filled with the smell, the best smell in the world.

His sister stopped him at the tea machine.

'You're waiting for Mam, aren't ya?'

'Yeah,' he said. 'Of course. Where'd you think I was off?'

She shrugged.

'I still can't believe it. Uncle Jack.'

He shook his head.

'I can't remember a moment when we haven't had Uncle Jack,' she said.

'He was hardly Uncle Jack these last few weeks.'

'I know but . . .'

Their mam appeared in the doorway, looking battered and bruised from the ordeal.

'He's in a better place now,' she said.

'Think so?' asked his sister. 'I just can't get over how quick it's happened. He was okay on my birthday.'

'Sometimes it's like that . . . for the best. We've known it was coming. He knew too. Can you get us one, love?'

Scottie leant back against the tea machine to steady himself. He was reeling inside.

'Yeah, sure.'

'We'll all have one, eh? I expect you'll be wanting to watch the game.'

'Mam!'

'Hey,' his mam said. 'Your uncle was the biggest Hoops fan this side of the river.'

'One for Uncle Jack,' said Scottie.

'That's right. Come on, forget the tea, I'll do us some up at home.'

'Good. It tastes like chicken soup here,' said his sister.

'It's that factory,' said Scottie. 'It gets into everything.'

They trooped out into the cold afternoon, Scottie and his sister on either side, their mam snug between.

'We'll sort the funeral for this week,' said his mam. 'I don't want you missing out.'

'It's just a holiday,' said Scottie. 'It can wait if has to.'

'It won't have to wait,' said his mam. 'You're going.'

Scottie smiled.

'Thanks, Mam,' he said.

They were at the bus stop. His mam had held it together throughout the whole campaign but now she crumpled under the strain. Scottie grabbed her to keep her upright.

'Come on, Mam,' he said. 'You've done so well.'

His mam looked up at him.

'What am I going to do without you?' she asked.

'It's just six months,' said Scottie. 'I'll be back in time for Christmas.'

His mam stared into his eyes.

'You make that a promise,' she said. 'Look me in the eyes and promise me you'll come home.'

'I promise,' he said. 'You know I promise.'

Things were happening quickly to Scottie now, altering and changing, people expecting things of him, unfaltering loyalty, responsibility, maturity, mad promises.

20

Scottie went straight to his room when he got home. He wanted to get out of his clothes. They smelled of the hospital and disinfectant and reminded him of his chemical warfare training, the thick charcoal-impregnated suit and respirator he'd learned to put on, the powder he had to apply to the suit to stop the chemical agents working. He was never any good at it. The instructors bellowed at him and made him do it again and again and in the end he just about managed it but he was all thumbs.

His uniform was hung neatly in the wardrobe. For a moment he let himself think about the next time he'd be wearing it but he stopped himself and blocked all of that stuff out. He had a million other things to do before then. In a few days time he'd be off on holiday with the lads. That was what he really wanted to think about, *all* he wanted to think about if the truth be told.

When he was changed he called Mackie on his mobile.

'You coming over? It starts in five minutes.'

'Yeah. How's your uncle?'

Scottie looked out of the bedroom window, down on to the yard and the shed at the bottom. An image fell into his head: one of his Uncle Jack hammering at the structure after a storm had ripped away part of the roof, his strong arms effortlessly driving the nails into the wood. By the end his arms had withered to nothing more than thin folds of skin and bone.

'I'll tell you when you get here,' he said.

'Okay mate,' said Mackie. 'Hey . . . five more days, mate . . . five more days . . .'

'You gonna get Drew?'

'Yeah, I'll drag him along. That's if he's not off with his latest . . .'

'He said he was coming.'

'Well don't hold your breath. He didn't turn up for five-a-side this morning.'

'You're joking. He never misses five-a-side . . .'

'He does now.'

'What's her name again?'

'Dunno. Becky I think.'

'What's he gonna be like on this holiday? We're gonna have to have words. You going to the offie?'

'Yeah, if you like. Just save us the sofa.'

'You've no chance.'

'You should be on the floor, getting used to roughing it.'

'Nah mate, I'm enjoying it while it lasts.'

The smell of chips and sausages met Scottie in the kitchen. His mam was bent in front of the oven, his sister sat at the table, sipping at a cup of tea, dunking a biscuit from the barrel.

'Mackie's coming over. Dunno about Drew though. He's got himself a new bird.'

'Not that Becky from the flats,' said his sister.

'Yeah, sounds about right.'

His sister shook her head. She was two years younger but she acted like he was the baby. His mam caught Scottie looking at the chips.

'They'll not be long,' she said. Then, to his sister, 'That Becky's all right. I know her mam.'

'It's 'cause she fancies Drew,' said Scottie. He grabbed a biscuit from the barrel and shoved it into his mouth.

'It is not,' said his sister.

'She always has,' said their mam. 'And leave those alone. I'm not making chips for nothing.'

'She's eating 'em.'

'She's not having chips.'

'I don't think I want one of your waster mates,' his sister shouted. 'I can do better than a school janitor!'

'Is that what Drew's up to now?' asked his mam.

Scottie nodded. He knew what she was thinking. She was wishing he had a job just like Drew, something just down the road, something she understood and would never have to worry about. It would be worse now Uncle Jack was gone. He was the only one who'd truly supported Scottie through the arguments, the only one who understood there was a world outside of the town. Terry would do his best to keep out of it all. He'd say his bit for sure but if the going got tough he'd crack open a tinnie and play with the TV remote, flick through the channels and pretend he was looking for some fishing show.

Scottie left his mam with the chips and went out back to the yard, ducking under the washing line on his way to the shed.

'Bring 'em down when they're ready,' he shouted. 'Pile on the sauce!'

'Fetch 'em yourself,' shouted his sister.

'You'll miss me when I'm not here.'

'Yeah, like a bad hair day!'

The shed was at the bottom of the yard. They'd built it together two summers before, Scottie, Mackie and Drew with Scottie's Uncle Jack in charge. They were fresh out of school and had nothing else to do with their days. They'd started without Uncle Jack, just the three of them. The World Cup was on and they wanted to watch the games but his mam and Terry were arguing every day about how they were going to cope with their money problems so the house was out of bounds. They started by clearing the rubbish heap at the end of the garden and went from there. Some of the stuff came from the council tip: old doors, tarpaulin sheets, chipboard and bits of shelving. They nicked some more of it from the local building sites, sneaking into the places after dark. Once his uncle saw they were getting their teeth into it he brought a load of wood and nails from somewhere and helped them get it sorted. They'd been making a right mess of it.

'You'd better hope it never rains,' his uncle laughed. 'And don't ever slam the door. The whole place'll cave in!'

He showed them how to set it steady and get the place rainproof. He fitted the electric sockets and wired them up to the house so they could rig up a light and an old TV and stereo. They got a worn-out sofa from Mackie's mam and two armchairs from a neighbour who'd chucked them out in the alley.

'They're almost new,' Mackie had said. He'd turned up breathless one evening having run to Scottie's the moment he spotted the chairs. Thirty minutes later they were sprawled out on them, blasting out tunes in their own little world. Since then they'd gone to town on the place, fitted a carpet and heater, got a portable fridge in there, rigged up a dart board and card table. It was their place, their domain and there was nowhere better. In the days when the shouting and screaming between Terry and his mam was at its worst, Scottie crept out of the house with his duvet and pillows, rigged up a bed on the sofa and slept there.

After a bit they got hold of a bunk-bed and fixed it up against the back wall. Now they slept there whenever they wanted. It was great after a night on the town. They could bundle in and crash about without having to worry. Mackie and Drew had the bunks and Scottie had the sofa. He'd tried the bunks but there was something about the sofa, something he shared with the thing.

Scottie stood in the doorway and flicked the switch. The shed filled with light, lit up the two-page-spread poster girls and Hoops players lining the walls. He went to the stereo and switched it on, opened the fridge and took out the last beer, got himself comfortable on his sofa and waited to see if Mackie would turn up with Drew in tow or if they were going to be taking the piss out of him from here to eternity for putting a woman first.

Lying on the sofa, his mind drifted once more to his Uncle Jack. Jack had been to the places and done all the things Scottie was about to do. It had made things easier in the first few weeks, just having him to talk to. Jack joked that the army was for softies these days and that it had changed beyond compare from when he was in, but Scottie knew there was a special thing between them. When Jack found out the news about his illness, how it was really taking hold, he'd come to Scottie first, even before he'd gone to Scottie's mam. He said it was best to hear things from the horse's mouth. He just came straight out with it, told Scottie he was dying and that there was nothing anybody could do about it. The two of them had gone straight down to The Thistle together and played pool for the whole of the afternoon, his uncle telling stories about the Falklands, talking about it all like it had happened yesterday instead of twenty years before. Afterwards, Scottie couldn't wait to get back to camp and crack on with it all. That was the thing about Uncle Jack. He had this way about him. When he spoke, Scottie couldn't help but listen.

After the game Scottie, Mackie and Drew spread themselves out across the place, slagged off the players who'd let the Hoops down and joked about who was fittest between the girls in *Loaded* and the girls in *FHM*, compared them to the lasses in the town. Mackie got to talking about work.

'I'm gonna try the Post Office. I fancy that. Outside in the sun and the rest of the day off when you're done.'

Drew cut in.

'I think you've to be eighteen to join the PO.'

'You're joking.'

'They're not gonna trust you with someone else's giro until you're eighteen.'

'There's nothing then,' said Mackie.

'There's the chicken factory.'

They all laughed.

'Me mam's always on about that place. No way!'

'It's full of drongos.'

'And Poles,' said Scottie. 'There's loads of them up there.'

'What about one of the call centres?'

'No way, mate! Andy went there. They trained him for a whole month! A month's training to answer the phone.'

'Is he still there?'

'Nah. He got the sack.'

'What for?'

'He told one of the managers to stick it. They were always on his case, for not selling enough, for not sticking to the script. In the end he tried chatting up some bird who phoned to complain about her washing machine!'

After Drew left Mackie asked about Uncle Jack.

Scottie shook his head.

'When?' asked Mackie.

'Early this morning.'

'Shit,' said Mackie.

'Trust the Hoops to play like that today,' Scottie said.

Mackie said nothing. He was looking at the nails in the frame of the shed, each one flush to the wood, holding the place together.

'It was nice and easy,' said Scottie. 'We knew it was coming.'

'I suppose,' Mackie said. 'Still shit though.'

'It hasn't sunk in yet. I was expecting him to stick his head in all the way through the game.'

'He'd have had something to say about that load of crap.'

'Dire,' said Scottie, mimicking his uncle's voice.

'Bloody shambles. Fairies the lot of 'em,' Mackie put the voice on too.

'No pride in the shirt. Too many foreigners. Not like it was in my day . . .'

They broke into laughter.

It was the best medicine.

Sunday coming to an end, the quiet time. Alone now, Scottie settled back on his sofa. He got to thinking more about his uncle, the way the drink had stolen his life away, first slowly and then with unrelenting speed. His mam wouldn't have it, though. They'd got to talking about it the day after his uncle had been rushed to hospital.

'Just because of the drink,' Scottie said.

'It's not the drink,' said his mam. 'It's everything else. The drink only happens because of everything else. Jobs. Money. Women. Being an ex-soldier. It all adds up. The drink's kept him going for a long time.'

Scottie went to the window and peered out of it. He thought about whether this was the right moment to tell her.

'Maybe it's this place,' he said.

'Not really. One place is as good as another,' said his mam. 'You see it on those TV shows all the time, people sloping off abroad, being just as miserable when they get there. They end up coming home in the end. It's not the place, it's what you make of it. Some of the happiest times of your uncle's life have been in this place. Then there's you and your sister. You two make him happy. He's always loved you in a special way, right from the start. He loves you almost as much as he loves the Hoops.'

Scottie's stomach lurched. It would have been easier if she'd blamed the city.

'Mam, I've something to tell you.'

His mam put the iron down, like she was waiting for something terrible. It made the moment harder. In the end he just came out with it.

'I've got my posting,' he said.

His mam picked up the iron again, went back to it.

'Well, thanks for telling me,' she said. 'But you might have tried to hide it better.'

'Eh?'

'You left all the stuff out on your bed. I saw it when I was getting your washing.'

'That was last week,' he said. 'You've known for a week?'

'I was waiting for you to say something.'

'So you're okay with it?'

His mam was about to say something but it was right then that they got the phone call from the hospital telling them they'd better come in. Scottie's mam had camped out at the place after that and Scottie had been up there every day, too. Now here he was in the shed, his uncle gone from the world, his mam holding on by a thread, hiding behind some shroud, and him signed up for a life that was going to take him away from all of it. He was going to change. He could feel it happening already, tiny alterations taking place, a new person growing inside of him. He put his head on the cushion and closed his eyes, thinking about the life he was about to leave behind. In an hour Mel would be over and they were bound to end up going through it all again. There would be the usual questions he couldn't answer because he didn't know the answers.

Three years before they'd wound up in the same PE group at school. Old Saunders had paired them up for a spell on the trampoline. It was stupid, done for a laugh or to prove a point, Scottie so big and Mel so small. At first they'd been clumsy, him using all of his strength to jump as high as possible, her hardly leaving the surface, hardly trying, just looking embarrassed, but she had this infectious giggle and she couldn't stop and that got Scottie laughing too. Saunders threatened to part them, told them to be serious, but his heart wasn't in it. He only threatened it enough to get them concentrating and when he did it was Mel who turned serious first, suddenly focusing on the task, causing Scottie to focus too until their timing fell spot on. It was like each of them were in front of a mirror then, the two of them landing on the trampoline as one, rising as one, falling as one. When Mel smiled at him, Scottie couldn't stop himself from smiling back. Pretty soon he was grinning from ear to ear and turning red in the face. When they stepped off the thing the rest of the class cheered. Even Drew and Mackie had cheered. They'd been inseparable ever since that afternoon, part of the fabric of the school, kids, teachers, dinner ladies all knowing about them, Scottie and Mel, Mel and Scottie, one name not meaning anything without the other.

Then school had ended and after a whole lot of nothing the army had come along, lit up his life, given him validity.

21

'**Turn it off,**' said his mam. 'I don't want to watch it.'

The whole family together in the living room, dinner plates on laps, knives and forks clinking, on the TV a reporter in the thick of it, ducked low in a ditch somewhere, mortar fire raining down on his position.

'It's a war,' said Terry.

'It's not a war. The war's over,' said his sister. 'They said on the radio.'

'It's never over. If it's over why are they sending my son there? Change the channel. I'm fed up of seeing it all. Stick something else on.'

His mam grabbed the remote and started flicking, changing from one channel to the next and the next until they were all looking at her instead. When she noticed she chucked the remote at Terry and got up out of her chair.

'Here, you have the damn thing. I'm putting the kettle on.'

'Make us a cup,' said Scottie.

'You'd best get used to doing it yourself,' said Terry.

His mam stopped in the doorway to the kitchen.

'Don't start that up again. He's not going. Did you see that? Would you want to see him in a place like that?'

'I'm going, Mam.'

'No, you're not.'

'Mam, it's my job.'

His mam looked at him, her eyes glassing over.

'You're not old enough to go,' she said.

Terry shot him a glance that told him to stop arguing.

'Bring us some biccies through then, Mam,' said Scottie.

'There's just choconobs.'

'Great,' said Scottie.

'I'll have one of those,' said Terry.

'You don't like 'em,' said Scottie and he laughed. 'Sit down, Mam, I'll do it.'

In the kitchen he filled the kettle and grabbed the biscuit tin from the shelf. He took a biscuit and ate it while he was waiting for the water to boil. He could hear them in the living room, trying to keep their voices down below the sound of the TV, his mam getting upset and Terry trying to get through to her.

'Talk some sense into him.'

'It's too late. He's done it. And anyway, he's old enough to think for himself.'

'He's not old enough.'

'If you felt like this about it you should have said something before he went off to training. Besides, it might be the best thing he's ever done.'

'I should never have let him do it. I knew this would happen.'

'Nothing's happened. Just wait and see.'

'He's not ready to go to a place like that.'

'He's been trained. What do you think the last six months was? What do you think that parade was all about?'

'Trained. It takes years to train for something like that. You can't train somebody in six months.'

'Well, they did,' Terry said. 'He's a soldier like the rest of 'em.'

'He's still my son,' she said.

'I know that, but he's not the same boy he was a year ago.

He's got skills now. He's got expertise . . .'

'Expertise! I'll bet he's making a mess of brewing the tea.'

'You're going to have to let go of him,' said Terry. 'Otherwise we'll have a right mess to sort out.'

'This is a mess,' said his mam. 'They're sending him to that place. It's all a mess.'

The sound of the kettle boiling drowned out the rest of the conversation. Scottie chucked the tea bags into the cups and poured the water. He added the milk how his mam and Terry liked it, carried the two cups through to them.

'I'm going to the shed for a bit,' he said.

'You can watch whatever you want in here,' she said.

'Nah,' he said. 'I'm going to have a kip.'

'At this time?' said Terry. 'Enjoy it while it lasts.'

It was a warm night, the air heavy though, a storm gathering. Halfway down the garden path Scottie stopped to get a feel for it, trying to work out the temperature, doing sums in his head and wondering how things might compare to the place they were sending him. In the shed he pulled on his headphones and turned up the volume. Things were threatening to get away from him. He wasn't going to pretend otherwise. Things were getting away from his mam too. There was nothing he could do though except block everything out, try not thinking about it until the day came around. The day for making choices, of really thinking things through, that day had come and gone a long time ago and, if the truth were told, neither him nor any of them had noticed its passing.

He was still lying there staring at the ceiling when his mam came out to see him. She had another cup of tea, more biscuits too.

'We're off to bed,' she said.

'Right,' said Scottie.

His mam put the tea and biscuits down, went back to the door, hesitated.

'You're going to do it, then,' she said.

'Mam,' he said. 'It's what they pay us to do, to go wherever they send us. We don't get to pick and choose.'

'I know,' she said. 'But I wish you did. I wish you could all just stand up and say you're not going.'

He laughed.

'Yeah,' he said.

'That's the last I'm going to say about it,' she said. 'From now on I'm keeping my big mouth shut. Are you coming in?'

'Later maybe,' he said.

'Will you be warm enough?'

'Mam!'

'Okay, sorry. Goodnight then.'

''Night, Mam.'

She closed the door and left him there on the sofa. He listened to her footsteps on the garden path, right up until he heard the back door shut, then he lay back and closed his eyes, not to sleep, just to immerse himself fully in the moment, to think and to practise not thinking because switching on and off like that was surely the key to the whole business.

22

It rained on the day of his uncle's funeral, low grey cloud smothering the cemetery, the pitter-patter of raindrops drumming on the coffin as it was carried from the chapel to the grave. They had to stand out in the rain when they sent Uncle Jack on his way, the pitter-patter drumming on umbrellas too. Sometimes the priest's words became lost amidst the sound.

Scottie had time to think about things at the bar in The Thistle during the wake. Strange faces he'd never seen before were all around him, faces that had come out of the woodwork in the days after his uncle died. His mind was on the last time he'd spoken to Uncle Jack, in the hospital just a few days previously.

The weather had been bad that day too, the sunlight smothered. His uncle looked frail and helpless in the hospital bed, like the bed itself was sucking the life out of him, but when he saw Scottie come in he lifted himself free a touch and wouldn't have it when Scottie tried to make him lie down again.

'I'm all right,' his uncle said. 'I can handle it.'

They got talking about the army almost straightaway, about how Scottie was shaping up. His uncle told a few tales of his own. Whenever the conversation threatened to veer away from the army to something else, his Uncle steered it back. Scottie knew he was heading some place with it all. He just had to wait and see. Eventually his uncle got to the Falklands and the mood in the room changed. There was no sound anywhere except for the hum of the air conditioning and his uncle's voice.

'There's nothing there. A few squat houses around some harbour, a few farms in the middle of nowhere. They dumped us on the shore and left us to get on with it but we didn't complain because we were the best and we had a job to do. You know what I'm saying. We yomped across that place like we were machines, up one mountain, down the next. There was a buzz all around, electricity fizzing between us, keeping us going. We were getting to do what we trained for. That was where the rush came from. You'll feel that. It's a great feeling. But it wears off in the end. None of us knew what doing our job meant, not really, not if we were truthful about it. In Ireland some of us had been shot at, some of us had done some shooting back, but out there we found ourselves in a real battle, close fighting, hand to hand, face to face, like nothing you'd believe.'

His uncle's voice was barely a whisper now. Scottie had to strain to hear it.

'When you kill someone,' said his Uncle. 'There's a moment just before it happens when you see your enemy and they see you. You both know what's coming.'

Uncle Jack pointed to his own eyes and then to Scottie's.

'I ended up in this ditch and there in front of me was a young lad, no older than the age you are now. He looked right at me and he knew what was about to happen, knew he was about to die. I had to do it. I had no choice. I was on automatic. If I'd waited even half a second he'd have killed me. But I didn't wait. I'd been trained not to wait. He just looked at me, looked right into my eyes. You wouldn't believe half a second could last so long. His eyes were full of the moment. I can see them now, wide open, staring right back at me, but I didn't wait. You mustn't wait.'

His uncle stopped whispering. He stared out of the window at the drizzle and rain, Scottie sitting there by the bed not knowing what to do with himself, his brain part-numb from it all. Then his uncle gathered himself.

'You'll see things that'll change you, Scottie lad,' he said. 'I saw one man fall on a petrol fire and burn up right in front of me. He was flailing around on the ground. None of us could get near him to help. By the time someone managed it he was in a right mess, screaming and screaming until he couldn't even manage that. Afterwards there was nothing left of him that you'd recognise.'

A bell rang in the hospital, caused Scottie to turn and look at the door. But his uncle didn't seem to notice it.

'When you see death like that, when you face your own death time and time again and somehow get away with it, when you have those things happen to you, see it happen to your mates, the same lads you trained with blown to pieces by your side, it's hard to come home and be normal just because everybody wants you to be. I know what your mam thinks of me but I did my best. I've had a life. Your mam doesn't know. She only thinks she knows and that's not the same. I'm not telling you this to scare you. You're not going to have to fight like we did. You'll probably do your six months and not see a thing. But listen, don't go looking for it. Do you hear? There'll be lads out there desperate to see some action but they don't know what that is. Keep on the straight and nar-row. Go out there, do the job they've trained you to do and get yourself home.'

His uncle rested his shoulders then, let his head fall back to the pillow and closed his eyes. Scottie sat with him until the nurse came in and told him it was time to go. He took one last look at his uncle before he left. This thin, frail man labouring for every breath was his Uncle Jack. It was hard to believe he'd been a soldier once, hard to believe he'd been as hard as nails.

They'd said their goodbyes to Jack but Scottie could almost feel his presence in the pub, in the pictures on the walls and the tankards hanging from the hooks above the bar, in the pool balls when they clicked together and in the dartboard when a dart thudded into it. Jack had been part of the place, part of its heart and soul. As long as there was The Thistle he'd be there. Scottie felt better for thinking it.

It was funny how you could believe one thing yet let yourself believe another.

23

A fair came to the city. It appeared like magic that weekend on the waste ground by the river. Scottie took Mel there. They went on all the rides together, had the biggest laugh. It was a release, a chance to get it all off their shoulders.

In an arcade he found her dropping money into a fortune-telling machine, one of the really old ones that just gave 'yes' or 'no' answers. He walked up behind her but kept his distance enough that she didn't see him. He watched her press the button and saw the word 'no' light up. She dropped some more money in and pressed the button again. It came up 'no' the second time, too. She was about to try for a third time when she spotted him. She looked flustered and went bright red with embarrassment.

'What were you doing?' he asked.

'Nothing,' she said.

He raised his eyebrows at her.

'I was just asking it some questions,' she said.

'What about?'

'Just stuff,' she said.

'What stuff?'

'Private stuff.'

'Tell me,' he said.

'No,' she said. 'It was private. Just leave it.'

'Tell me,' he said again.

She turned on him.

'I said leave it,' she shouted. Then she turned from him and walked out of the arcade.

'Hey,' he shouted back at her. 'Hey, I've just got change.'

But she wasn't listening. It took him half an hour of trailing behind her, at a distance because he knew her well enough, first through the fairground and then along the path by the river, before he could get any sense out of her and it took him another two hours of joking, teasing and playing the fool before he got her back to how she was when they'd first set off for the fair. He wanted to ask her about the fortune-telling machine to find out what questions she'd asked it but he didn't want to start her off again so he kept his mouth shut and just acted the clown, showering her with compliments, tickling her, brooding when she didn't respond with a smile. Eventually, she cracked, and joked that he was acting like a love-struck teenager.

'I am a love-struck teenager,' said Scottie.

'Since when have you used the word "love"?'

'Since now,' he said.

She stopped laughing, looked at him seriously for a moment while he kept a straight face staring back at her. Eventually, she dropped her eyes from his.

'The army's meant to toughen you up,' she said. 'Not make you soft.'

'You've been on at me for ages to say it.'

'Only because you used to say it all the time.'

'Aye,' said Scottie. 'When I was fourteen. When we first got together. Now I say it and you're funny about it.'

His heart was racing, his guard down. He didn't know what to do with himself.

'I'm not used to it,' she said.

'Well, it's been a weird few weeks,' he said.

She was harder to be with all evening after he'd said it, forever looking at places where he wasn't, lying on the sofa with her back to him, letting him close to her but not in the usual way. When she was asleep, he started wishing he hadn't said it but there was nothing he could do. It wasn't something you could say and then pretend you hadn't said and it wasn't something you could take back either. He made a decision that he'd not say it again. It made no sense to be thinking that way but it helped him get to sleep.

The next day he kept his distance until she was her old self again, giving him cuddles when he didn't want them, all of that stuff, but it was no use pretending things were back to normal because they weren't. Things were changing between them in all sorts of ways, some for good and some for bad. Or maybe it was all in his head. Maybe it was simply knowing he was leaving her. Whatever it was he didn't like it. He felt guilty about the holiday, too, and thought about how he could make things better for both of them. It wasn't going away with the lads, she was supportive of that as only Mel could be, but it was not making the most of the time they had left together. That was the thing. She wasn't saying anything but she had to be feeling it because he was beginning to feel it and she was always, always a step ahead of him, always treading the path he was about to tread, feeling things he was about to feel, knowing things he would surely come to know.

In the last couple of evenings before the holiday he avoided the subject, hoping she might say something, not having the nerve to do it himself. But she didn't say anything. She helped him pack instead, made sure he had everything he needed, didn't once raise a point about the unfairness of it. Eventually he cracked.

'Do you want to come?' he asked her. 'We could still get you a flight.'

'What and spend a week with you three together? Just me? You've got to be kidding.'

'We could squeeze you into the flat.'

She stuffed a folded pile of his boxer shorts into his suitcase.

'I couldn't come even if you made a reasonable offer,' she said. 'Work's too busy.'

She zipped his suitcase shut and stood it up in front of him.

'Besides, it's a good trial run,' she said.

'Trial run for what?'

'When you're away for real. If I can't last a week, what chance have I got with six months?'

Scottie dropped his gaze to the car park below the window. It was still empty. He wondered how that could be. Hours had passed since the thing began outside the nightclub, over half a day, more than enough time. It was not playing out the way he'd expected.

The girl was crying softly. She'd been that way for an hour, ever since he'd wiped the smile off her face by forcing her into the corner. She'd tried to speak, had come out with a load of gibberish about knowing she'd find him in the school, how she'd seen him on the train, how she wanted to help but he'd told her to shut it and in the end she'd done just that.

His shoulder had started up again, pulsing and throbbing, and he was thirstier than ever, his throat parched and sore. Stabs of pain shot through him each time he swallowed. He rested his back against the wall. He was uncomfortable on the wooden floor but he'd experienced worse, much worse. This was a holiday.

He surveyed the scene in front of him, the classroom, the barricaded door, the girl. She was a real problem. He'd not bargained on her. But he could not risk letting her go. There was too much at stake. The girl pushed her legs out in front of her and dropped to her side, still crying. It couldn't be helped. Detachment was the key. It was what they had taught him, not to let his emotions get in the way, to stay focused and get the job done. The pain came again, a dull throb that caused him to slump forward and feel for his shoulder. He closed his eyes and waited for it to go away. To distract himself he took a peek out of the window.

He could see the hill and the trees of Tanners Park on the horizon. He thought about the day he and Drew had gone running up there together, back when all of this was just beginning. He thought about Drew's asthma, thought about how a bad thing could become a good thing in the blink of an eye. The trees were sitting in softened grey silhouette against the afternoon sky, the whole of the Hillside estate spread out below them. This was his kingdom. He could survey it all from here and take comfort in the fact that nothing had changed. Everything was as it should be. Everything was in its place. He wondered how he had ever come to be anywhere else.

24

It was the first time any of them had been abroad, the first time any of them had been on a plane. Scottie had only ever seen the place in the brochures they'd picked up at the travel agents and on the TV. With its clear blue skies and swimming pools it looked too good to be true.

He paid the most out. He was flush after training so he set the money down for the three of them. Drew gave him some when he got his pay from the school but Mackie had nothing. He kept going on about how he'd pay Scottie back, how he wouldn't let him down and what a great mate he was.

'Shut up about it,' Scottie said. 'I know you're good for it. Just give it to me when you've got it. You don't have to keep making promises you can't afford.'

'But I'll get you it,' said Mackie. 'You can have my giro on Thursday. That's eighty quid straight up.'

'You'll need that for spends,' Scottie said. 'You can pay me when you've got a proper job and some proper money.'

'That'll be never then,' laughed Drew.

'I'll get something as soon as we get back,' said Mackie. His face was reddening and his eyes widening, the way they did when things got to him.

Drew stuck the knife in.

'Yeah, and the Hoops'll do the double this season,' he laughed.

Just then the 'fasten your seatbelts' light pinged on and the pilot's voice echoed through the cabin.

'Quite a light-show out of the right-hand windows,' he said. 'Some heavy thunderstorms so please stay in your seats, belt up and expect a little bit of a rough ride. The weather in Portugal is fine so once we're through this it's happy holidays.'

One or two people cheered but Drew went quiet. Mackie spotted it straight away. He turned to Scottie.

'What happens to a plane if lightning strikes it?' he asked. He was trying to look serious but behind his eyes he was grinning from ear to ear. Scottie picked up on it and joined in.

'It'd cut the plane in two, mate. Like opening a tin of beans. We'd just spill out.'

'We're sitting ducks up here,' said Mackie.

Drew pretended not to listen, his fingers locked on the arms of his chair, his back pressed against the seat. Scottie and Mackie stared at each other in mock horror and Mackie started pretending to bite his fingernails.

'Such a couple of jokers,' Drew said at last.

While Mackie stared at Drew and Drew fought to ignore him, Scottie turned his face to the window and watched the spectacle, the lightning coming in bursts, lighting up the sky like shellfire. Every now and then the plane shuddered. Scottie looked around him. It was quiet. Most of the passengers had fallen into themselves, into the places they visited when the world threatened. Some had iPods hooked up to their ears, others had their heads stuck in magazines and books. Some were sleeping. It was hard to imagine they were heading out for holidays they'd worked all year for.

The plane landed in the early hours.

'This is it, lads,' said Drew. 'Let's get the party started.'

He started dancing, spinning in circles while they waited in the baggage queue.

'You boys need to wake up,' he said. 'I say we get to the flat, get changed and head out clubbing.'

'No chance,' said Scottie. 'I'm whacked out.'

'Save it for later,' said Mackie. 'We've a week. I need my kip.'

'You're a couple of sad tossers,' said Drew. 'Suit yourselves. I'll head out on my own.'

The transfer coach was air-conditioned but it didn't cool Drew down. A gang of girls were sat at the front and when the lads got on Drew sat himself down amongst them. Scottie and Mackie went to the back out of the way.

'Like a dog on heat,' said Mackie.

'Aye,' said Scottie. 'An ugly one, too.'

Ten minutes later Drew came waltzing down the coach to join them.

'They're staying in the same apartments,' said Drew. 'What a result!'

He rubbed his hands together.

'You're unbelievable,' Scottie said.

'And you're just jealous.'

'We've hardly arrived,' said Mackie.

'Yeah, but it's dog eat dog out here.'

Mackie and Scottie shared a look.

'So what are their names?' Scottie asked.

'See! See!' Drew laughed. 'Where would you boys be without me?'

For the rest of the journey they shared ratings, telling each other which one of the lasses they'd be going for. Whenever Scottie piped up Drew and Mackie took turns in reminding him that he had Mel at home.

'I'm only looking,' said Scottie. 'There's nothing wrong with looking. Besides, what about Becky?'

Drew looked quizzical.

'What about her?' he asked.

The coach made its way through the darkness, orange lights marking their path along the coast road. Every now and then it stopped. The rep at the front shouted the name of a hotel and little by little the coach emptied until there was just the three of them and the six lasses.

'Two each,' whispered Mackie.

'Are you kidding?' said Drew. 'It's three for you and three for me. He doesn't get any, remember?'

The rep took them into their apartment building and helped them get sorted. They let the girls go first so by the time they made it up to their room it was nearly morning.

'Still off out?' Scottie asked Drew.

'I'll give it a miss this first night,' said Drew. 'But only tonight. After that it's hard partying for seven days straight. No excuses.'

When they finally got sorted and in their beds dawn was breaking. Scottie lay in his bed waiting for sleep to come. He watched the light change beyond the window, watched it grow bolder and fight its way through the fly-screen. The thing about Drew was that he never stayed faithful long enough to let anything mean something. He'd been like that since he was fourteen, always jumping from one lass to the next.

Scottie took out his phone and sent a text to Mel, to let her know he was thinking about her. Then, knowing he wouldn't be sleeping any time soon, he went to the balcony to watch the sunrise.

25

After a morning sleeping and an afternoon by the pool they made their way into the town through the narrow streets, following the music, following the crowds. The air was heady, suntan lotion mixed with burgers and chips, perfume, alcohol. There were girls everywhere, gaggles of them, dressed in next to nothing. As the lads walked, their eyes jumped from one set of legs to another.

'I've died and gone to heaven,' said Drew.

'Imagine wearing that back home,' said Mackie. 'She'd freeze her bits off.'

The knick-knack stores were still open and they bundled their way through them, knocking into carousels, ducking under shirts and swimwear, skipping around decorated plates and baskets. They grabbed a table outside a restaurant and stuffed themselves with steak and chips, washed down the lot with lager.

'Better than The Thistle,' said Mackie.

'The promised land,' said Drew.

He raised his bottle.

'A toast to Scottie,' he said. 'For the best idea he's had in eighteen years.'

Mackie lifted his bottle to Drew's and then Scottie lifted his too.

Scottie grinned.

'To dosh,' he shouted.

'Aye, to Scottie's dosh,' shouted Drew and Mackie.

There was having money and not having money and there was no way on earth that the second could ever be better than the first.

26

They lost track of the days. One late afternoon they found a bar with a big screen and settled in their seats to watch the Hoops. They filled the table-top with pints of lager, three each to save going up to the bar once the game started.

Mackie sipped at his first pint, half-way down the glass already, leaving the other two behind.

'Jesus, pace yourself,' said Scottie.

Mackie belched.

'I can handle it,' he said. 'I'm not expecting you two to keep up. You couldn't if you tried.'

But they weren't in the mood to try. The game was kicking off. More and more lads flooded into the pub. There were Hoops shirts everywhere.

'It's like The Thistle,' said Scottie.

'Aye, but with a better view,' said Drew.

Scottie turned around to face the sea. The sun was dropping now, the sky turning pink.

'Aye,' said Scottie.

'Not there, you soft git,' said Drew. 'There.'

He pointed to a gang of girls at the bar, on some pub crawl, dressed up as nurses, all tanned legs and high heels, stockings and garters.

'That's a view,' said Drew.

Throughout the game the lads in the bar chanted football songs and the girls sang songs of their own, the whole thing fuelled by alcohol and sex, the girls parading their wares, up on tables and chairs, flashing bits of themselves at the lads who flashed bits back until the game on the screen became an after-thought. It didn't matter that the Hoops were waltzing it back home. Each time a goal went in, the place erupted and then all attention fell back on the girls. Drew went to the bar and came back with six lagers and a blonde in tow.

'This is Abby,' he shouted. 'She's a nurse.'

'No way,' shouted Mackie. 'I'd never have guessed.'

The girl screamed with laughter.

'Do you want examining?' she snorted. Alcohol came up through her nose and she ran in the direction of the toilet.

Mackie looked at Drew.

'Nice one,' shouted Mackie. 'Real class.'

'Who cares?' Drew shouted back.

'Tell her you'll see her at the club,' said Scottie. 'I need to get some scoff.'

'Go get it,' said Drew. 'If you think I'm letting her out of my sight for one minute you're having a joke.'

'You already did,' laughed Mackie. He pointed across the bar. The blonde was sandwiched between two topless lads, bumping and grinding to the music.

'Jesus,' said Drew.

'Are you coming?' asked Scottie. 'Or are you going to sit here pining?'

'Aye, I'm coming,' said Drew. 'I'll catch up with her later.'

'Like she'll remember you,' said Mackie.

'Of course she'll remember,' said Drew. 'Nobody forgets the Drewmeister in a hurry.'

27

On the beach, Drew staring at gangs of girls, Mackie busy with his music, Scottie flicked through a newspaper, heading for the sports section but getting distracted along the way. The headline read:

British Soldiers Killed.

Mackie spotted it too.

'What did they teach you about dying then?'

'Eh?'

'When they were training you.'

'They didn't teach us anything. They don't teach that.'

'They should. They should give you lessons in how to do it properly, otherwise you might make a mess of it.'

He laughed.

Scottie closed the paper.

'They train us how to stop that happening. That's the whole point.'

'Doesn't always work though, does it?' said Mackie, pointing at the paper. There was a picture of a burned-out vehicle and two portraits, fresh-faced lads in parade uniform staring out of the page.

'Shut it, Mackie,' said Drew.

He flicked sand on to Mackie's stomach where it stuck to the suntan lotion. Mackie spat some lager at Drew in retaliation.

'How can you drink that at this time?' asked Drew.

'Hair of the dog, mate. Have you not heard of it? It's what us men do.'

Drew shook his head, then changed his tune.

'Hey, she's looking over again. It's the one from the bar last night.'

'She will do if you keep staring. She probably thinks you're stalking her.'

'She wishes,' said Drew.

The two of them went on at each other while Scottie finished the article.

'Says it was a road traffic accident,' he said at last. 'That can happen anywhere. You don't need to be in the forces.'

He looked up from the paper to see Drew and Mackie off up the beach towards where the girls were sat. After a moment he turned over and started with the problem pages.

It was mid-afternoon when the aircraft appeared. It came in low and fast over the beach, performing some sort of show for the crowds, the sound of it coming first, appearing out of nowhere, offering no warning, no time to prepare. In a flash it was upon them, just above the surf line. People stopped what they were doing to look up at it, confusion written on their faces. The surge and power of the engines pressed down upon the beach and the noise was deafening, a thunderous roar that ebbed and flowed as the aircraft turned back and forth into and out of the breeze. It climbed steep, impossible climbs and turned at shuddering angles, defying gravity and propulsion. It was beautiful and precise and elegant but full of aggression and ferocity. The adults on the beach stared up in wonder at it. The children stared too but some were scared by the noise and started to cry.

'Jesus,' said Drew. 'I just want to chill and look at the lasses. If I was into plane spotting I'd be off in an anorak some-where.'

Scottie felt nervous about the plane. At first he thought it was a fear of the thing coming crashing to earth because when it turned it seemed to stop in mid-air and if the breeze carried the sound away it simply seemed to be hovering unbelievably above their heads. He imagined it falling out of the sky, crashing down upon the beach. But it wasn't really a fear of the thing crashing. The angry snarl of it, the speed of it, the way it could turn so quickly, got him thinking about what it was designed for. Mackie had the same idea.

'Imagine that thing opening up on us now,' he said.

Scottie's stomach lurched. It was a perfect killing machine. In his head he'd always thought of it differently, aircraft screaming by, bombs, death, all of those things, but a random thing, down to fortune, the chance to run away and find cover, a chance, always a chance. But there had been no time to react. The plane had simply materialised in the blink of an eye, a black monster in a perfect blue sky. And this was just a display. In war it would be carrying death and destruction on its wing. The thought of it remained with him through the rest of the afternoon, long after the plane had disappeared and the rhythm of the beach had restored itself. In a daydream the aircraft came screaming over the sand out of nowhere. The sand became a desert. He was running blindly, going nowhere. There was nowhere to hide, no escape. Bullets fizzed past his ears, sprayed up the sand, thudded into his flesh and muscle, tore him to pieces.

Unable to shake the thought, he left the shade of the lounger, tiptoed his way across the hot sand to the water, where the sand was wet and cool. He stood at the water's edge and let the sun work through his body until he felt energised by it and then he walked into the sea. The water was cold on his skin at first. It numbed his toes and ankles but he waded on until the water was above his knees, his toes sinking into soft sand and then on some more, breaking through the waves as they came at him, forcing his way through them to the calmer water beyond. When the water reached his shoulders he started to swim in lazy strokes, enjoying the heat on his face and the soothing cool of the water whenever he submerged. He rolled over on to his back. The sky was perfectly blue. He could hear the screams of laughter around him, children playing at the surf line, husbands and wives, families. He thought about the other lads from training, how they were preparing themselves. He wondered if they were coping better than him. Then he thought about his Uncle Jack.

On a day not long after the selection course, before he got the details of his basic training, he'd slept out in the shed on his own. He woke not long before lunch and was raging hungry so he went across to the house to dig out some grub. His mam was still at her morning cleaning job, Terry serving at The Thistle, his sister at school. He was expecting an empty house but there was a voice coming from the living room. Uncle Jack. He popped up like this all the time and his mam always gave him the sofa when he did. Scottie whacked some toast under the grill, then went over to the living room door. He was going to barge in and rugby-tackle his uncle to the ground but at the last second he stopped. There was something in his uncle's voice that didn't sound right.

'I don't know,' he was saying. 'Next week some time. He just said further tests. I think I know what it is. I can feel it.'

A pause.

'I know I shouldn't but it's true. Anyways I'm glad for the boy but I hope he knows what he's letting himself in for.'

Scottie's body stiffened in the hallway. He strained to listen more closely. The house was deathly silent, just his uncle's voice cutting through it, a hollow, muffled sound beyond the door.

'He'll see things, things that might change him, things that make everything else different.'

Somewhere far off, so slight it hardly registered, Scottie could hear a thin voice on the other end of the phone. He wondered who his uncle was talking to. He was witnessing a side to his uncle that he'd never known before, a taste of the man behind the myth. This was his Uncle Jack, ex-para, Goose Green veteran.

'I know. I know, but nobody was there to tell me. That's the difference. Anyways I'll see you later. No, no, not yet. I'll speak to him when he wakes up.'

When his uncle went quiet, when it was clear that the conversation was at an end, Scottie retreated to the kitchen. The toast was burned on one side. He had to throw it away and start again. He was slapping margarine on the new slices when his uncle came through. He had a cigarette between his lips and a can of lager in his hand but he didn't try to hide them, just placed them on the side and gave Scottie a hug.

'Wee man,' he said. 'How's it going?'

'Great,' said Scottie.

'I hear you've got some news.'

'Aye,' said Scottie.

'Following in your old uncle's footsteps, eh?'

Scottie shook his head.

'It's not the paras. It's nothing like that.'

'Well, you've to start somewhere,' said his uncle.

He broke into a coughing fit then, doubled over with it.

'I wish you luck,' his uncle said at last. 'Now, how's the hut holding out? Better than me I hope.'

'You'll be all right,' said Scottie. 'Too many of those things, that's your problem.'

His uncle flicked some ash from the cigarette into the sink.

'You're maybe right,' he said.

But he went to the fridge next and took out another one of Terry's lagers.

'Are you having one?'

'Nah, I've just woken up,' said Scottie.

'That's the best time for one,' said his uncle. 'The best way to kickstart the day.'

They went outside and stood looking at the shed from the back steps, talking about the Hoops mostly, Scottie waiting for his uncle to say something about the army, waiting for him to have the words he'd mentioned to whoever it was on the phone but his uncle said nothing, nothing at all until the day in the hospital months later.

Scottie came to his senses when Drew and Mackie bombed into the sea either side of him. The three of them fought each other in the surf, late afternoon sun colouring the water and the sand, the beach slowly emptying of people, day replacing night, the party showing no signs of letting up.

28

A market place, puddles of water on the ground, smouldering black frames of burned-out vehicles, pandemonium, bodies on stretchers, ambulances forcing their way through crushes of people, black smoke rising.

'It's mental over there,' said Mackie.

They were sat in a bar staring at the TV, music pumping out, no sound on the TV but no sound necessary. Scottie said nothing. He was looking at the men in the crowd, trying to read something in their faces.

'You're going to be right in the middle of that,' said Mackie. 'You're mental.'

He was drinking vodka in shots, one after another.

'That's not where I'm going,' said Scottie. 'It's not like that where I'm going.'

'I hope you're right,' said Mackie. 'For your sake.'

Scottie was red in the face, from the heat of the afternoon, from the lager and from the way Mackie was acting about everything.

'It's not worth it, mate,' said Mackie. 'It's not worth this holiday, not worth having a car, not worth that flat you and Mel keep on about. It's not worth any of it.'

'It's worth not having to sit on my arse at home,' said Scottie. 'It's worth not hanging around outside the jobby with a bag of chips. It's worth those things.'

'All I'm saying is we could stay here,' said Mackie. 'We could have this every day. Why do we have to go back? Why does Drew have to go and clean up chewing gum from carpets? Why do you have to go to a place like that? We can get jobs here, have a laugh, do this every day of the summer and work in a bar surrounded by lasses every night.'

'It's not that simple. There's Mel for a start.'

'Get her over here, too,' said Mackie.

'She wouldn't be up for it,' Scottie replied. 'It's not her thing.'

Mackie's glass was full of vodka again.

'Do you believe in friendship?' Mackie asked. He had a cigarette on the go, his eyes half-shut against the smoke.

Scottie shook his head.

'What? What are you shaking your head for?' asked Mackie. He flicked ash on to the table.

'What sort of a question is that?'

'Friendship. Looking out for each other. Brothers. All that?'

'Aye. You know I do.'

'Then don't go,' said Mackie. He took a long drag this time and his eyes were fully closed as he said it.

'You're talking like I have a choice,' he said.

'You're an idiot,' said Mackie. 'A complete idiot. Drew too. Except he's just a lucky idiot.'

Scottie downed the rest of his pint.

'Nothing's gonna happen,' he said.

'Right,' Mackie said. 'Life's just like that.'

'What then? What do you suggest? Go back home. Get a job in the chicken factory, spend the next twenty years there?'

'It's better than dying,' said Mackie.

'It is dying,' said Scottie. 'It's dying like the rest of the sad bastards, slowly, with nothing to look forward to.'

'There's Mel,' Mackie said.

'Mel understands.'

He paused for a second until he knew Mackie was waiting on his words.

'Mackie, this is your scene. You'll fit in. You suit all this but it's not for me.'

'What more do you need? You can get a job, keep your tan topped up. Coming here was the best thing we ever did.'

'Joining the army was the best thing I ever did. And don't forget what paid for this trip.'

'I haven't forgotten. That's what all this is about. You want to talk about forgetting, you need to go and find Drew. One sniff of skirt and he forgets everything.'

Mackie broke into laughter. Scottie smiled back at him.

'I was about to lay into you then,' said Scottie.

'Aye,' said Mackie. 'That's the army for you. Hit first, discuss later.'

They started back to the apartments, Scottie and Mackie in front, Drew behind with the girls he'd cracked on to.

'This Mel business. They don't want you getting married, you know that?' said Mackie.

'You what?'

'The army. They don't want you married. They want to keep you single.'

'You're mad, you are.'

'I'm right, mate. That's the truth of it. If you're single you're cheap and they can afford to lose you.'

'It doesn't work like that.'

Drew came up to them.

'Will you two boring bastards shut up about the army,' he said. 'It's all I've heard for three days!'

He was slurring his words and they ignored him until he dropped back to the girls again, carried on with his banter, stuck his arm around the blonde of the bunch. She didn't do anything to push him away. Mackie shook his head.

'He's unreal,' he said. 'Pissed as a fart and they still let him maul them.'

Drew's voice rattled on behind them.

'He's off in the army next week. He needs one of you to give him a proper send-off!'

He was pointing at Scottie, the girls peering ahead, trying to work out which one Drew was talking about. Mackie pointed to Scottie to make it clear.

'Now he's starting on about it,' said Scottie. 'Jesus!'

The words fell out of his mouth. They were sadder than he'd imagined. They were darker too. It was like emptiness, like he was standing on the edge of a sheer cliff. His future was clear. It was just about stepping towards the cliff edge and not thinking about what was out there waiting for him. He was good at it, really good at it, or he had been until the last few days. Now everything was about where he was being deployed. There was never a moment when he could escape it. Even when nobody was talking about it he could see it in their eyes, a silent, invisible fear gnawing away. It was in Mel's eyes when she kissed him, in his mam's eyes when she brought him his morning tea, in Mackie's and Drew's eyes all of the time, all the way through the holiday. Unable to escape his own thoughts, oblivious to what Mackie was saying to him, he started running, knowing it wasn't the answer but doing it anyway. Mackie shouted after him and started running too, but he gave up after a few steps and stood there holding his sides. Drew shouted but the girls were laughing and his voice got lost in the cacophony. He heard one of them yell, 'Hey, we won't bite you,' and Drew shout, 'Bite me instead,' but he didn't look back.

He ran to the end of the strip, dodging the clubbers as they stumbled out on to the street, dodging the scooters and the taxi cabs. His steps fell in pace with the heavy bass sound from one club and when that sound faded another took its place.

On and on he went, up the hill, moving on to the tarmac road, running on the white line because there was no pavement. There were no people either. The road switched back on itself then switched again. Soon he was up above the town, the lights below, darkness above, cicadas chirping amongst the trees. He started to feel sick, felt it boiling up inside of him, jumped the metal barrier, bent himself double just in time. He let it come. A taxi passed and somebody shouted something from out the window. Scottie watched its lights disappear around the next bend, his stomach in knots. When the worst was over he started up the hill again, heading for the apartment. He wanted to go home, to get his bags packed and get on with it. The sooner he was out there in the thick of it the better, because here, here in this no man's land he was in danger of losing himself.

At the apartment Scottie stood on the balcony looking down over everything. It was the middle of the night but the air was warm like a summer day in Calton. He could hear the laughter and screams of the lads and lasses having the time of their lives. But something had changed in him and something was stopping him from being like them. It had started in the job centre during that first interview, a feeling of separation, of being different, and it had grown slowly from that moment to this, through the whole of the previous winter while he waited for his start date. Then there had been the training. The things he'd learned.

All of that had taken another part of his old self, replaced it with this new being he was struggling to live with.

He was starting to feel different about Drew and Mackie, especially Mackie who seemed to be going further and further off the rails as the weeks went by, but Drew too, in smaller ways, things like his way with the girls. He didn't understand why something like that, something that was nothing really except about having a laugh, something Drew had always done, should suddenly make him feel anything. But it did. The feeling made him uncomfortable. He wanted to cling to the things they'd had the last ten years, the life they'd shared, but he knew it was getting away from him and he couldn't cling on forever. Memories came to him across the darkness, carried on the beat of the music, each one a complete moment. Mackie as Joseph in the nativity play back in primary school and him as the grumpy bar-keeper. His mam sat in the front row as he played the part, shouting about not having any room in the inn, about how much they'd have to pay for using the stable. Judith Presley as Mary. Mackie hating it because he had to hold her hand every day in rehearsals and then hating it even more when he had to hold her hand in front of the whole school. Judith Presley, who had left and moved to the Isle of Mull with her parents, sent the whole class a card that first September back. Inside she'd written, 'To Class 5A, especially Mackie Roberston.' A row of kisses beneath. Their teacher stuck it on the notice board for all to see and the class thought it hilarious. Drew and Scottie playing up front together for the school team against the rival school from across the way, Drew skinning their defenders and laying on Scottie for a hat-trick, the two of them diving belly-first into the mud at the touchline, Mr Heath not being able to hide his pride and joy at being the first teacher to beat their rivals in twenty years. The school assembly the next day when they'd got Scottie and Drew up at the front, Mackie rolling about on the floor in a fit of laughter. The three of them taking the piss out of the supply maths teacher at secondary school, tying her up in knots with their antics, sending her from one corner of the room to the other for books and pens and set-squares, sending her around in circles, reducing the woman to tears, not giving a toss about it.

Now he was leaving them to go to a foreign place. He was scared. It was that simple. He'd tried to hide it by talking up the training and talking down the place he was going to and what was going on there but the truth was different. He was scared of the unknown world they were sending him to, scared of what was waiting for him. He was scared of things not being the same when he got back. They were growing up, growing apart, taking different paths. It was what happened. There were all these things to fear and then there were the biggest fears of all, the ones that came every day, the ones he was still trying to cope with like getting injured or getting killed. Most of the lads looked at these things in the same way though some were more scared by the first than the second. Whatever, the best thing to do was to not think about them. It wasn't worth worrying unless they happened and when they happened it was too late.

Scottie hopped off the balcony and on to the fire escape, followed it down and around to the poolside. The lights were still on in the pool, the pattern of the blue tiles shimmering on the bottom. He took off his shirt and dropped it on one of the loungers, took off his sandals too so that he was just wearing his jeans and nothing else.

The stillness of the pool attracted him. He didn't want to break the spell so he entered the water gradually, trying not to produce a single ripple or sound, making out that he wasn't really there at all. He waded until the water was at his knees, his waist, his chest, steered a path through the water, letting it swallow him until it was at his chin. He felt the ripples flatten and settle, raised his arms gently until they were extended at each side of him, the tips of his fingers brushing the surface of the water, the water clinging to his skin. He stood still until there were no ripples, until the water resembled a solid form. The water was at his mouth. He could feel his bottom lip beneath the surface, his top lip exposed to the warm night air. A feeling came over him then, came with absolute clarity, a feeling that he was being watched. He turned his head to take in all four sides of the pool. There was nobody, yet the feeling remained. He held himself in position a moment longer, concentrating hard and then in a perfect smooth motion he stepped into deeper water. The water swallowed him. The quiet of the poolside was replaced by the sound of the filter humming, bubbles rising and popping at the surface, his beating heart. He held his breath, surprised at how easy it was, and counted the seconds, testing himself, testing his nerve, thinking about the training for the gas attack, trying to do better and when the first wave of nausea came he forced it away. He could beat it. There was no sergeant in his face this time, no recruits watching and waiting their turn. He relaxed and let his body cope with the change. It was easy. The humming of the filter faded, carried all other sounds with it until there was nothing at all, just the blue of the walls all around him, the spotlights, and then a small blurred figure at the edge of the pool, a child staring down into the water, a girl, the blue of a perfect sky behind her, a beautiful garden, the colours of many flowers, olive trees, perfect shade, the colours of the garden running together, the picture losing all meaning, running to black.

Terror enveloped him. He sucked for air and his lungs filled with water. He thrashed about, chlorine burning his throat, struggled, fought his way to the poolside where he dragged himself clear clumsily, losing his grip, fighting the sluggish heaviness of his being, his head full of misshaped images.

A child?

A blue sky?

A garden?

Scottie collapsed on the concrete, coughed up the contents of his lungs. Pool water flooded from his mouth and nose. There was a pounding in his head, a full-on cacophony of sound and behind it all he could hear shouting, shouting that grew in volume and resonance. When he rolled over on to his back he saw that the hotel manager was standing over him.

'Hey! Hey!'

Scottie got himself to his feet, backed away and ran, pathetically in small steps, fighting to keep his balance as jolt after jolt of pain exploded in his head, trying not to slip on the tiles surrounding the pool, his feet slapping on the slabs that came after. He made a grab for his shirt and sandals, pulled them to his heaving chest, all the while nodding and apologising to the man who followed him to the foot of the stairs, shouting words in Portuguese as he made his way up the fire escape to his room.

When Scottie got to the room he let the screen slam behind him, grabbed a towel from the bathroom, folded himself in it and went back to the balcony. He stood leaning on the rail, letting his skin dry, expecting the manager to re-appear. When nothing happened he stepped back into the room, collapsed on to his bed and closed his eyes.

A garden?

A child?

He fell asleep thinking about them.

Later, after Mackie and Drew had crashed in and woken him before collapsing into their own beds, Scottie went to the bathroom. He stood in front of the mirror and examined his reflection. He was unfamiliar with himself, unfamiliar with the thoughts in his head, with his physical being, his level of fitness, his readiness. It was all new to him. He walked through to the bedroom and dropped on to his bed again, tiredness crawling over him. Mackie and Drew were sleeping already, Drew on his back, his arms straight by his sides like a corpse on a slab. Scottie had never been able to get used to it. He had fears of Drew drowning in his own vomit, had thought about it on nights like this ever since he'd learned Drew slept that way. He watched Drew's chest, kept his eyes open until he was sure he could see the steady rise and fall that meant Drew was still alive and then he let himself go. As he passed from waking to sleep the most vivid picture formed in his mind.

His head filled with the image of the garden again, a perfect blue sky, a sea of flowers, enticing shade. There were rocky outcrops, huge round stones like table-tops sitting by entrances to caves, people gathering in the shade to sit together and whisper of events he did not know of. Peace settled over him. It was like coming home to a place and remembering it and never wanting to leave it.

29

'I bet he's got some half-baked idea in his head,' said Drew.

It was the last morning of the holiday. Mackie had left them in the apartment and wandered into town. Half an hour before the coach pick-up, he still wasn't back.

'I'll see what's taking him,' said Scottie.

He shot down the street, taking the flight of steps between the buildings three at a time, and found Mackie sat at a table in the place where they'd started most of their evenings.

When he saw Scottie he made sure he got the first word in.

'What happened to you last night?'

'Eh?'

'Running off. What was all that about?'

'I just wanted to get back,' said Scottie. 'I do it all the time at home. Did you know you run faster when you're drunk?'

'It only feels fast,' said Mackie. 'It's an illusion caused by being pissed.'

Scottie sat down and waited for Mackie to say something else but before anything got started Drew turned up.

'Jesus, what are you playing at? Come on!'

'I'm not coming,' said Mackie.

Drew turned to Scottie.

'Told you,' he said.

'Told you what?' Mackie asked.

Drew sighed.

'Told him you had some idea in your head about finding your own little place in the sun.'

'And?' Mackie asked.

'Mackie, we've been on holiday. It's all right if you're on holiday. There's nothing to do all day except drink beer and lie back with the sun on your face. But staying is different. What are you going to do for money?'

'I've a job.'

'Don't tell me,' said Drew. 'That kebab shop on the corner where you've spent most of the week.'

'Funny,' said Mackie. 'I've a job in a bar, glass collecting.'

'What about a place to stay?' Scottie asked.

'All sorted, mate. There are rooms for staff on the top floor. If I do a full shift they feed me twice, once at the start and once at the end.'

'A full shift?'

'Twelve midday till close.'

'That's hours, mate. These places don't shut till three in the morning!'

'I don't care,' said Mackie. 'It's better than home. There's nothing there. What am I going to do? I've been chatting to some of the others. They do a summer here and then they head for the slopes and do the winter in the ski resorts. I can do this all year long if I want.'

'Don't you need papers?' Scottie asked.

'The guy at the bar says he'll sort that. He says if I do the rest of the summer he'll hold the job for me next year. Says he'll get me behind the bar too if I work out okay.'

'Yeah? Well those blokes'll say anything,' said Drew.

'Come and get the coach,' said Scottie.

'No. I'm all right, mate. You head back to your miserable weather and I'll stay here working on my tan.'

He stopped after that, knowing it wasn't worth pursuing, got up and marched back towards the apartment. Scottie and Drew watched him go.

'I can't believe it,' said Scottie.

'I can,' said Drew. 'I had a feeling from the start.'

'Yeah, I know what you're saying but I didn't think he'd actually do it.'

'No?' said Drew. 'I've been watching him all week. I've seen it ticking over in his brain. And do you know something?'

'What?'

'I think I'm jealous of the bastard.'

Drew made like he was going to say something else and then changed his mind. He got to his feet.

'Anyway, whatever he decides we've got to get that coach or you'll be AWOL before you even begin.'

'Chance would be a fine thing,' said Scottie.

On their way up the hill Drew got it out of his system.

'It's been a good week,' he said. 'I'm glad we did it even though I'm gonna be skint for a month.'

'We'll do it again next year,' said Scottie.

'You reckon?' Drew asked. 'You'll be married this time next year.'

'So what if I am?' Scottie said. 'What difference does that make?'

'Are you kidding? What world are you living in?'

30

Flip-flops were priceless out in the desert. Mel took some days off and the two of them spent the last few days of his leave on shopping trips for stuff like that, stuff the lads said he'd do well to have.

They spent every night in the shed on the sofa. Sometimes, when they weren't laughing and playing around, when he wasn't teasing her, when what was coming took a stranglehold on their thoughts, there were long bouts of silence. He tried to fill them with jokes and antics but he couldn't always think of something in time. Some of the silences were so difficult they argued with each other just to fill them.

On the last night he took her to the Cineplex. Because the weather was okay they walked along the river together. He tried to make it special but something was on her mind. When they reached the benches he stopped her.

'What is it?' he asked.

'What's what?'

'You.'

'It's just this whole thing,' she said. 'We've had the best week but now we're saying goodbye again. It only feels like yesterday that you got back from training.'

Scottie turned away from her and looked down at the water, brown beneath the overpass. Mel sat on the bench beside him, not saying anything and he couldn't think of anything easy to talk about so in the end he just launched straight in.

'It's just six months,' he said.

Nothing.

'When I come back I can afford to take you away.'

He reached to put an arm on her shoulder but she forced him away.

'It's always going to be the same. Six months here, six months there. We'll hardly see each other. What's the point in being together if we hardly see each other?'

'I thought you didn't mind,' he said. 'When I signed up you said it was okay.'

'Yeah? Well that's before I knew how bad it was going to be,' she said. 'When you go away it isn't all fun and games, you know. It's fine at first, just me and the girls down the pub having a laugh. It's okay at the club too, for the first hour, then they all catch up with their blokes and I'm left tagging along.'

'What about Danielle? What about Kirsty? They've not got blokes.'

'Usually off snogging in a corner somewhere. Me on my own.'

'Rachel then. Her bloke works on the rigs. He's away all the time.'

'Yeah, but she's different. She's not bothered about going out. She likes staying in with her feet up. I like to go out with my man and go home with him. Some chance of that these days.'

She stopped talking and turned to face him again.

'Why can't you just pack it in?' she said.

'Pack it in? Just like that? Just go in on Monday and tell them I'm quitting?'

She did nothing, nothing at all, just sat there.

'I can't. It's not that simple. Even if I wanted to I couldn't.

It's not like any other job. They'd arrest me. And there's the lads . . .'

He saw the way she looked at him, the futility of trying to explain it.

'There's nothing to be scared of. I'll be okay.'

'That's not the point,' she said. 'I mean it is, I'm scared for you, of course I am so that's part of it, but that's not what I was talking about. I'm scared for me. Six months is a long time.'

'What's that meant to mean?'

'Nothing,' she said. 'Nothing. It's not meant to mean anything except what it is. Six months. Six months without you. Six months without us!'

'These things don't come around that often. We get loads of time at the barracks, months and months. Once I get back, once I get settled and get some time under my belt it's not that different to any other job. Honest. It's five days a week and the weekends off. I've looked into it. Just think about it. When I come back I'll be able to drive. I'm nearly trained now. I'll be getting some wheels. I can take you to places. We can go to the outlet centre whenever you want. No more buses. No more old folk nicking all the seats. Play some tunes on the way.'

She smiled. When he saw it he grabbed at it and milked it some more.

'It'll work out,' he said. 'You've just to get used to it, that's all.'

'Spend my Saturday nights watching *X-Factor* with Rachel?'

'I thought she was one of your best mates.'

'She is. But you know what she's like. It's all Alex this, Alex that.'

'Great,' he said. 'You can talk about me to get her back.'

She smiled a vacant smile.

'It's not forever, just six months. After that it'll be easy.'

He pulled her close, felt her begin to come back to him.

'I just don't want to miss you,' she said. 'I hate it.'

'I hate that part too,' he said. 'Sometimes I wish I'd never bothered. I should have took that job at the factory.'

'The chicken place? You're joking. If you took a job there that would be the end. That's a promise.'

She laughed and he laughed with her. He thought about clocking in at the chicken factory each morning, working his hours on the production line, heading home brain-dead in the evening. He wondered what his mam was thinking trying to get him to go there, but he knew what she was thinking really. She was thinking that the chicken factory was just about as safe a place to work as existed, but she didn't understand. The army was dangerous and there was a risk of something bad happening but a few weeks in the chicken factory would have really meant the death of him. The chicken factory sucked something out of people, a little bit of something each and every day. Some of the crowd up there, the ones that could switch off, were okay. They went to work, earned their money and came home the same. They split themselves in two somehow, became one person at work and another at the end of the shift. They did okay for themselves, got married and had kids, all the usual stuff. He didn't have a problem with them.

It was the ones who hated it there that frightened him. The lads who'd been like him in the years above him at school. The jokers and the clowns who'd ended up there because there was nowhere else to go. The ones who dreamed about escaping but couldn't be arsed to do anything about it. They festered. He'd seen it happen to others too, bright lads who were just going there for a few months, just until something better came along. A year later they were still there but the spark had gone from their eyes. They hung around the pool table at The Thistle each night, smoking. They stared at the football games on the screens, sunk too many lagers, got fat, stumbled around the corner to Jimmy's kebab place at closing, hovered around the gambling machine munching on kebab meat until Jimmy closed up. Then they went home for six hours of kip before the next shift. Every time he ran into one of them they talked about how the next time he saw them they'd be doing something else and the next time he saw them it was the same, and the next time and the next until eventually the subject never came up, he just knew they were still at the chicken factory. He could see it lurking somewhere behind their eyes.

Mel understood. She was going somewhere. She was going to get her qualifications and then she was going to start her own business doing home calls or go and work for one of the salons in the city centre. A lot of the girls at school had said the same but a lot of them had quit their training already. Not Mel. She was going to do it. It was one of the things he admired her for. When she said she was going to do something she did it.

'I don't want to feel like this,' she said at last. 'I like telling people you're a squaddie for a start. It's dead sexy. You should see the lads in the club when I tell them. You should see their faces. Like rabbits in headlights.'

'You shouldn't be talking to lads in clubs,' he said with a grin.

She looked him in the eye. There was a glimmer there.

'It's just window-shopping,' she said.

'At least you can do that,' he said. 'I have to share a tent with a bunch of pig-ugly blokes.'

'That's how it should be,' she said. 'Do you think I'd let you share a tent with a load of lasses?'

'I could window-shop,' he laughed.

'Window-shopping's something girls do,' she said. 'Lads don't know how to window-shop. They always have to buy something.'

She got up to go.

'Come on,' she said. 'I'm hungry, aren't you?'

'Starved,' he said.

'Can't we just go back?' she said. 'Get something at home? I want to be with you tonight, not sit staring at a screen. We can walk back the way we came.'

She held out her hand and he took it.

'You know you said we've had the best week,' said Scottie. 'Well, it can be like this all the time from now on.'

'You reckon?' she asked.

'I've got a million ideas,' he said.

'Better than the outlet centre?'

'Miles better,' he said.

'What like?'

'They're secret. You'll have to wait and see.'

They wandered along the riverbank, each slow step carrying them closer to the moment he didn't want to happen. After a few minutes she stopped again.

'Here,' she said. 'I want you to have this.'

She was holding something in her fist.

'What is it?' he asked.

She opened her fingers and dropped it into his palm. It was a silver St Christopher on a chain.

'Patron saint of travellers,' she said. 'In case you don't know.'

'Of course I know,' he said.

'It was my dad's,' she said. 'He gave it to me.'

'I shouldn't take it then.'

'Of course you should,' she said. 'It's you that's doing the travelling, not me. Unless you count walking up and down Hillside to work every day . . .'

He put the chain around his neck and she fastened it, then she kissed him. Together they continued along the path by the river. Up ahead, behind the tower blocks at the top of Hillside, dark clouds were rolling in, swamping the estate, swallowing the orange sunset, altering the picture they were walking into.

They spent the night in the shed together. It was their place and neither of them wanted to be anywhere else.

Scottie woke in the small hours to the sound of rainfall spattering against the roof. He lay for a long time listening to it, Mel sleeping quietly beside him, thinking things through, going over them again and again and again. There was no way out though, no way of changing the course of things. It didn't matter how afraid he felt or how scared Mel was, didn't matter how much they were going to miss each other or how difficult it would be. It didn't matter what Drew thought or his mam or anybody. All that mattered was the army, the job he had to do and getting focused one hundred per cent because if he didn't, if he couldn't do that, he was a liability to the other lads and a liability to himself.

The splattering got heavier and heavier until it was raining like there'd be no tomorrow to worry about, rain hammering on the roof and pounding on the windows. Thunder followed. He lay listening to it and it made him nervous. Mel stirred but Scottie shushed her, held her close to him.

'On the holiday, on the beach, there was this aircraft . . .' he whispered.

Mel stirred beside him.

'What?' she murmured.

'It doesn't matter,' he said. 'Go back to sleep.'

It rained and rained until water started dripping through the roof and on to the blanket. He covered Mel's eyes with the edge of it, reached over and switched the light on. Sure enough water was gathering in one place, growing heavy and dripping down. He watched the drips for a minute, checking their regularity. In the past he'd have grabbed a bucket from the garden, stuffed it down there, closed his eyes and ignored it but tonight was different. He was different. He'd learned there were better ways to do things. He slipped out of the blanket instead, went to the box in the corner, got himself a hammer and nails and some of the plastic sheeting from under the bunks. He remembered his uncle leaving it there, saying it might come in handy in the future. Not bothering with a jacket, not even bothering to get dressed, Scottie stepped out into the rain. He clambered on to the roof and set about sorting the problem. Sure enough, the plastic seal had started to come away, was flapping to and fro in the breeze. Water was getting underneath it. He placed the new bit of plastic over the old bit, got it into position and then started hammering nails into it, securing it, mending what was broken. That was the thing, to just do it, to get it done and to do it the best you could. It was simple. He stayed out there in the rain, the rain soaking his skin, washing away the last remnants of the boy in him.

The hammering woke half the street. He saw his mam's light come on and saw her come to the bedroom window.

'What are you playing at?' she shouted.

'Fixing the roof.'

'It's three in the morning!'

'It needs doing. There's water coming in.'

'Come inside then. Leave it till morning.'

'I won't be here in the morning,' he said.

Back in the shed he dried himself off and let Mel fall asleep in his arms yet again, then unable to sleep he slipped off the end of the sofa and wrote a letter to her. He didn't say much, just told her the things she already knew, that he was going to miss her, that she was special to him, that he'd think of her each day and that when he got back he'd treat her to the best day of her life. And he tried to put his reasons into words too, not the stuff about the chicken factory because she knew that, but the stuff about the lads he'd trained with, the stuff about feeling part of something, of having a whole set of brothers to work with and look after each day, about how they were the reason he couldn't just jack it all in and step away from it, how he'd never known a feeling like it, never known a closeness like that, even though sometimes they were a million times different from how he was. When he was through he put the letter in an envelope and slipped the envelope into the pocket of his jeans.

That was it, the final act of a life he'd been growing for eighteen years.

31

He walked Mel through the estate to the hairdresser's, feeling hollow inside. He was tired, in all sorts of ways, had hardly slept after the roof episode, just spent the rest of the night staring at the place he'd mended, his mind in overdrive, his stomach forming ever-tightening knots.

The two of them said their goodbyes on the step up to the shop door, repeating things they'd said already, making promises, wishing away the months that lay ahead, the months separating them from their future together. He took the letter out of his pocket.

'What's this?' she asked.

'Open it later,' he said. 'After I've gone.'

'You're not dumping me, are you?'

He laughed. They kissed for one last time and then she was gone from him, the door swinging to a close, her racing past the other girls towards the back room. He turned away, started back up Hillside, his feet dragging, his head a mess.

When he got home his sister was sat at the kitchen table munching away on breakfast cereal.

'Shouldn't you be at school?' he asked her. 'Again!'

'I'm waiting to see you off,' she said.

'Any excuse.'

She went on munching.

'Enjoy it while you can,' she said. ''Cause tomorrow you'll miss me.'

He went to the fridge, grabbed the milk.

'Don't drink from the carton,' she said. 'That's disgusting.'

He stopped, looked at her over his shoulder. She was mirroring her mam, already on the way to becoming her. With him out of the place there was going to be fireworks, the two of them sure to go at it. Scottie grabbed a glass off the sink, poured the milk into it and put the carton back. His sister smiled.

'Don't push it,' he said. 'You know Drew's picking me up in his new wheels to take me to the station.'

'You mean he can drive? Isn't there a written test for that?'

Scottie swallowed the last of the milk.

'You should have more respect,' he said.

'What, like you did when you were at school?' said Claire. 'I told Mr Groves you were in the army now. Know what he did? He laughed and said you wouldn't last five minutes.'

'Well, he got that wrong.'

'He said you did nothing the whole time you were at the place.'

'What does he know?'

'He taught you for five years!'

'We just went and got registered then hid behind the sheds.'

'Did you hear that, Mam?' she shouted. 'You have a go at me if I miss a half-day!'

Their mam's voice sounded from somewhere upstairs.

'That's because you know better.'

Claire whispered at Scottie.

'You know Mam doesn't want you to go?'

'It's a bit late for all that.'

'So you're going whatever?'

'I don't have a choice.'

'What about Mam? What about when she starts missing you?'

'Tell her no news is good news.'

'It's me who's left to sort it out,' said his sister.

'For a minute I thought you were thinking about someone else and not yourself,' said Scottie.

'I am thinking of someone else. I'm thinking of Mam and Terry and everybody. You'll be all right out there. You'll know what's going on. We're the ones left in the dark.'

Drew turned up twenty minutes later, spinning his car keys in his fingers and grinning from ear to ear.

'Let's see these wheels,' said Scottie.

He gave his mam and sister a kiss in the kitchen, not making a big deal out of it, just doing it, moving out of the kitchen in the same motion. His bags were stacked in the hallway, waiting.

'Is that all you're taking?' asked Drew.

His mam laughed.

'It took him the whole of yesterday,' she said.

Scottie hoisted one bag on to his shoulders, grabbed the second with his free hand and chucked it at Drew who dropped it, surprised by the weight.

'You're kidding me,' said Drew.

'You need to get down Frank's gym,' said Scottie.

He said his last goodbyes. His sister came to the door as they started down the path but then she saw Scottie winking back at her about Drew, making like he was going to say something, so she ducked out of sight. She was at the net curtains in the living room window when the two of them pushed through the gate and out into the estate. Scottie's mam came to the door in her dressing gown, waved and shouted at him until he reached the alley that ran to the parking places.

'I thought they'd be all tears,' said Drew as they slipped out of sight.

'Not my sis. She's too tough. My mam will be though. She's been up and down all morning.'

'It'll fly by,' said Drew. 'Think back six months. We'd not so long been for that medical.'

'Aye,' said Scottie. For a second he did just that, drifted back to the time before the army.

'I guess you're right,' he said.

Drew clicked his keys and an alarm beeped on a blue Saxo in the car park.

'What do you think?'

Scottie nodded. The car still needed a bit doing to it but it was better than he was expecting. He felt a stab of jealousy but it passed in a shot. When he came back he'd have enough in the bank to get his own.

'Smart, mate,' he said. 'Really smart.'

Scottie climbed into the passenger seat and watched his friend slip in behind the wheel. The inside smelt of wax and polish. There wasn't a speck of dust to be seen.

'You'll never keep it up,' said Scottie.

'When you come back you'll be begging me to take you out in it,' said Drew. 'This is the Drewmeister's latest weapon. The perfect pulling machine . . .'

Scottie laughed. He was still laughing when they passed the school. Up on the top floor some kid was half-hanging from a window.

'Remember when we used to do that?' Scottie asked.

'They're not meant to open up there,' said Drew. 'But the kids pull the safety catches off. They're on my list to sort. I'll screw them shut. That'll stop 'em.'

'You'd best hurry before he falls out,' said Scottie.

'Be one less to worry about,' said Drew.

'I don't know how you can stand to walk through those gates,' said Scottie. 'It'd take something to get me in there again.'

'You know how I feel about it, but it's a job mate,' said Drew. 'It'd be all right if it wasn't for the kids. I spend two hours cleaning the stairs and the next day I go in it's like I never did it.'

They talked cars for the rest of the journey, Drew explaining his plans for neons and spinners, Scottie nodding one minute and shaking his head the next, arguing the toss, but as they ran out of things to say about cars nothing came to replace them. In the end Drew turned the radio on to blast away the silence but even that didn't help.

'You're not saying much,' he said.

'I'm okay,' said Scottie. 'Just thinking, that's all.'

'What about?'

'When I get back, you're still gonna come over to the hut, right?' he asked.

''Course I am, mate. You know, you're the lucky one. It's me who's got to stick around here. It's gonna be crap without you and Mackie.'

He gripped the steering wheel with both hands and drummed his fingers, staring at the car park through the windscreen. Tiny drops of rain were falling on to the glass.

'I found out what was eating Saunders that day outside school.'

'Yeah?'

'Yeah,' said Drew. 'But I don't think you should hear it.'

'I want to hear it,' said Scottie. 'You can't say something like that and then not let me hear it.'

Drew hesitated.

'Go on,' said Scottie. 'Before the train comes.'

'I was cleaning some graffiti off the walls in the stairwell behind the hall,' said Drew. 'Saunders was there on his break. He just started on about it.'

He hesitated again, saw the look Scottie gave him, sighed and went on with it.

'He asked about you, told me they used to have the army come in to school to talk to the leavers. He was in charge of it all. It was something he did before they made him Head of

Geography. The army came every year. It was just another careers thing like all the rest. He didn't think anything of it. One year they had three lads sign up.'

Drew looked up at Scottie again.

'You know what I'm going to say,' he said.

'It doesn't matter,' said Scottie. 'I want to hear it anyway.'

Drew sucked a lungful of air between his teeth.

'Some lad signed up and about six months later he got himself killed in Ireland,' said Drew. 'Saunders blamed himself, for having the army into school and putting the idea into the lad's head. He stopped inviting them after that. He said he was going to say something to you at the gates but then I turned up and he lost his nerve. He told me to tell you to keep your head down.'

Scottie grimaced.

'Aye, well, there's always stories like that,' he said. 'They told us a few in training, showed us pictures and everything. I'm going into it with my eyes open.'

'He's right though, mate,' said Drew. 'Keep your head down.'

'Don't worry,' said Scottie. 'My head'll be so far down I'll be sniffing my own farts.'

They both laughed, filling the car with it and then, right on cue, the train turned up.

'I'd best hurry,' said Scottie.

He jumped out of the passenger seat and went to the boot for his kit. He was well laden with the bags as he ran to the platform.

'See you then,' shouted Drew one last time.

'See you later,' shouted Scottie, but he didn't look back. He couldn't bring himself to do it. He didn't want to have a moment that stuck in his mind, not with any of them. So far he'd done all right and got it over without much fuss.

When he got on the train he chucked his kit into the rack and stuck his iPod on. It stopped him thinking. Whenever an image of his mam or sister or Mel tried to find its way into his head he swapped it for whatever he could see from the window, whether it was the green landscape, a busted-up estate or the black emptiness of a tunnel.

32

The days before embarkation were manic. They flashed by in a whirl of preparation, lads on last-minute fitness regimes, lads doing the opposite, heading off into town to get pissed night after night. Some of the older blokes recorded themselves reading bedtime stories for their kiddies and then got Scottie to show them how to burn copies so they could record other messages for their wives.

Before he knew it Scottie was out on the square with the rest of them, waiting for the buses to come and carry them away. In the half-light lads were huddled in small groups, smoking or making last-minute calls on their mobiles. Scottie made his way through them, picking his footsteps carefully, looking for familiar faces. Most of the lads were sorting through their things, kneeling and squatting under the lights, opening bags and compartments of bags, rummaging through them, zipping them shut, remembering something else, sorting and checking again.

Scottie spotted McDonald and made his way over. He was sat on his pack, smoking, looking pissed off. When he saw Scottie he perked up a notch.

'I didn't know you smoked,' said Scottie.

'I don't,' said McDonald. He laughed, lifted the cigarette up to his mouth and took another drag. 'You all set?' he asked.

'Ready as I'll ever be,' said Scottie.

'Aye, that's about it,' said McDonald. He looked around

him at the lads who were busy with their bags. 'I forgot razors,' he said. 'All week I've been telling myself to get razors and I still forget 'em. But we'll be able to get them out there, right?'

'Dunno,' said Scottie. 'I've got some anyway. I'll give you some when we get there.'

'Cheers, mate,' said McDonald. 'How do you feel?'

Scottie shrugged his shoulders.

'Me too,' said McDonald. Then he threw the cigarette down and stamped it into the tarmac.

The buses sped them through the night to the airbase. Scottie stared out of the window, watching the world he knew slip away, the orange lights retreating one by one, his eyes following them until he finally began to drift, hypnotised.

At the base they swapped the buses for an aircraft. Scottie climbed the steep steps one at a time, boots clunking on metal. He ended up sat next to some lad he'd never spoken to. Once they were up and had just the flight ahead of them the lad shut his eyes. Scottie did the same. He slept for one hour more, forgetting where he was, drifting off into memories.

When he woke the lad was reading a small Bible. A lot of the lads had dug them out in the last week, lads that never said anything about that sort of thing, lads that hardly read at all. When the lad went to the toilet, Scottie picked the Bible off the seat and leafed through it, trying not to rip the thin pages. He tried reading a bit, something about men building a tower and God not liking it, but he didn't really understand it. He gave up on it after a minute and put it back. He spent the rest of the flight trying to get back to sleep and failing. His head was full of what the next few hours were going to bring, his stomach tight. Lads were visiting the toilet constantly. He went three times himself, splashing water on his face, staring at himself in the mirror, trying to see if he looked scared, trying to find expressions that made it look like he wasn't.

33

There was nothing to see when they came into land save for a few lights scattered sparsely across the landscape. A cheer went up when the wheels touched down, there was a collective intake of breath that said 'let's get the job done' and then each and every one of them were sent sprawling by the heat as they stepped into it. Scottie caught up with McDonald on the tarmac.

'Jesus,' said McDonald. 'I'm sweating buckets already. What time is it?'

'Five in the morning,' said Scottie.

By the time they boarded the vehicles to take them to the buildings, thin strands of light were bleeding over the walled edges of the compound. The lads battled to find their bags amidst the piles and then they were taken off to their quarters. Scottie collapsed into a heap the moment he was given a bed, hardly caring any more about the place he'd arrived at. The closeness of the heat had knocked the stuffing out of him. Most of the lads stripped to their boxers and groaned about how they were never going to cope. Scottie felt his wet skin sticking to the bedding and wondered the same. It made the heat of the holiday feel like a winter day at home and it wasn't even morning yet, the sun hadn't even started to do its work on the place.

There were stag duties and briefings, briefings and stag duties. In between they slept, ate, checked and cleaned their weapons, the checking and cleaning mechanical, part of their very being. For the first few weeks they were too knocked out to do anything else. They lived behind bastion defences of solid concrete surrounding the compound, walls and ceilings two feet thick and they didn't venture beyond. Boredom was their biggest enemy. The lads had dust-covered flags of St Andrew hanging from the little windows, showing their colours. Every now and then they took one down to get the dust out and the colour back in.

Life was dominated by routine. Even the mortar and rocket attacks became routine. Routine to dive for cover and keep your head down, routine to stay put and wait for the explosion, routine to do that with your heart in your mouth until the all-clear sounded, the fear of death so constant and pressing that eventually there was nothing to do but grow accustomed to it and live with it. They were forced to make the best of it all, forced to wait out the time between stagging on by re-telling their life stories.

'I'm from the Highlands, right up near Loch Shin,' said McDonald. 'I grew up on a sheep farm. It's hard these days and there's no money in it but it's the family business. I was always going to carry on the farm so I didn't bother with school. I was always around the farm working on the machinery. That's what I'm good at. I'm going to do my ten years and then I'm going back. If I play my cards right I'll have a few quid in my pocket by then. My dad won't change things, that's his problem, but farming's like everything else these days, you have to move with the times. Tourism's the way to go. It's great country where I live. People will pay a price to see it and live it. I'm going to convert the old barn, maybe grow organic, get the trendies up from Edinburgh. They'll pay more. I might have a kiddies' farm too, a few lambs and goats.

Rabbits are good. I can wander about in my later years and tell stories about the old days when I was in the army.'

'Some fun that'll be,' said Scottie. He put on the voice of an old man. 'One day I did four hours' sentry duty staring at a concrete wall . . .'

'Aye,' said McDonald. 'Well, what are you going to do?'

'When I get out? I've only just joined!'

'So have I, but you've got to have a plan, otherwise you're just drifting from one day to the next.'

'There isn't much going on in Calton.'

'Calton?'

'Aye.'

'You poor bastard. No wonder you joined the army! "He gets shot at less now than he did at home!"'

Laughter with Scottie at the centre of it, but he wasn't going down without a fight.

'Hey,' he shouted, 'your name's McDonald and you live on a farm . . .'

'Aye,' said McDonald. He looked to the heavens, already knowing what was coming before it started.

The lads piped up as one.

'Old McDonald had a farm . . .'

'I've never heard that one before,' shouted McDonald.

'Really?' shouted Scottie. 'Come on then, lads!'

'Old McDonald had a farm . . .'

The lads creased up. The clock ticked on a notch.

'I was always going to be a soldier,' Atkinson told them. 'I knew it since I was eight when I joined the scouts. I went on summer camp year after year, learned field craft. Every year when I came back my mam said I looked like a soldier. I couldn't keep out of trouble at school. When I was ten they stuck me on tablets for ADHD. They calmed me down and I was on them all the time after that. I only stopped taking them two years ago. I had to be clean for two years to sign up. I drove the teachers mad when I stopped. They all wanted me to go back on the stuff. Even my mam wanted it. But I wanted the army more than that, so I had to learn to control things. I did it. I got through it. I made it. I'm here. In this place. What a joke.'

He started grinning, grinning so his teeth showed.

'What a disaster.'

The lads only laughed at his story when Atkinson laughed. He demanded a certain respect from the others without saying anything about it. He earned it by the way he approached everything, the way he carried himself, the way he spoke. No matter what the task, he did it exactly by the book. Whenever Scottie felt down, far from home, fed up with everything the army wasn't, Atkinson reminded him of what the army could be. But it worked the other way, too. Sometimes Scottie felt inadequate next to Atkinson, like the army was meant for Atkinson and Atkinson was meant for the army and that was the sort of person the army really wanted, not him.

Eventually the lads came to be looking at Scottie. He told his story as it was with no fancy attachments and missed nothing out. He told them about his uncle and the Falklands, The Thistle, Drew and Mackie, his sister, his mam, Calton, the estate, the chicken factory. Nobody laughed when he finished. You could hear a pin drop. For a minute he thought they were serious then they burst into fits of laughter and took it out of him for being such a depressing tosser.

The only lad that got away with not telling was Colton. As Scottie's turn came to an end and the threat of the moment happening became real, Colton crept silently away and out of the door. Scottie watched him go. He didn't say anything. Everybody knew Colton was best off keeping himself to himself. Everybody knew it was best to leave him alone.

One day leading into the next, the lads counting the days gone and the days to go. Stag, briefing, fitness and football

before the sun got truly up, poker, rest, sleep at night, sometimes sending a message home, the camp in the middle of
nowhere, their whole world limited to what they could see
from its walls. Things would change when they were shifted
to patrols. Weirdly, Scottie found himself hoping for that day
to come. Stagging on was getting to him. He spent most days
at the back gate, bored out of his head.

Each day the men came to sign up for work, forming a line
against the wall below him, boots shuffling forward in the dust
at no pace at all, talking quietly, smoking their tobacco, occasionally looking up at him but mostly watching the road junction, listening for the sound of a rogue vehicle, holding their
place in the line, not wanting to leave it, not able to leave it,
but always one eye trained on the junction, never forgetting
where they were or the risk involved. They were just ordinary
men hoping to support their families, trying to survive.

Scottie was the same, watching and waiting under the hot
sun, with time to think. The worst thing about stag was having time to think because that was when the fear came. The
two were inseparable. Sometimes he felt like a wild animal,
one of the weaker kind at the bottom of the food chain, one
that had to spend its entire life expecting the next minute to
be its last, always on guard, always nervous, always under
threat.

So there were just the hot days melting into one another,
dust in the gutter, dust on the queueing men, sometimes coming in little swirls that danced and formed patterns in the air.
But the swirls only came when there was a breeze and there
was hardly ever any breeze, just the heat and haze, the road
block at the junction a distant blur. Sometimes when a car
passed the haze played tricks on him, so that it seemed the car
had melted straight through the road block and was heading
for the compound and the line of men and even if he was
ready, even if his mind was set on the task and not wandering
back to the streets of Calton, not thinking about Mel at all or

Drew or Mackie, he wouldn't have time to stop it, wouldn't have time to train his rifle on the driver and get a few rounds in, or even if he did the momentum of the car would take it straight into the compound wall beneath him, straight in to the line of men. There would be a deafening explosion. There would be carnage.

Sometimes, stagging on at night, he pointed his rifle at shadows. The space beyond the compound would become enveloped in threatening darkness. He'd flick the safety catch off. His finger would twitch on the trigger. Stray dogs lurched amidst the concrete. Strange, horrifying sounds emanated from the blackness, sounds that caused him to imagine unspeakable things being done by one human being to another, so that he was forced to whisper to himself to protect his imagination from hearing.

He needed a change before he lost his mind. After eight long weeks of numbing repetition, the change came. They moved into the barracks, took the places of those before, started on patrols. It was new and exciting and dangerous too but at least he felt alive again, like he was finally doing something useful, like he had a purpose being there.

34

Dusk settled over the camp and brought the first signs of a storm with it. A thick cloud rolled in, blotting out the redness of the sun, softening everything. Shadowy forms emerged and dissolved away to nothing as the dust thinned and thickened, ghosts of soldiers, without features or edges. At one stage a pink darkness swallowed the place. It sounded impossible, but staring from the doorway Scottie looked straight into it, though even as he thought about it, so it changed again and again, found another shade, moved, twisted, clotted until the camp was engulfed once more.

The lads coughed as the dust got trapped in their throats. There was always somebody coughing. After they coughed they swore under their breaths, then they coughed some more. Scottie couldn't stand being cooped up. He pulled on his goggles and stepped outside to escape. Immediately the dust found every part of him.

There was not much to see, just the ghostly outlines of two helicopters sitting uselessly on the earth, the shadow of the mess tent, red-brown clouds of the storm hiding everything else. He stayed out for another ten seconds until the dust covered the goggles and made them useless too and then he went back in. He kept the goggles on for a moment before lifting them from his face, wet a finger with his lips and ran it across his forehead, wandered over to the mirror that was strapped to the post in the corner. Atkinson was giving him the hard stare.

'Keep the damn door shut,' he said. 'There's dust enough.'

And then Atkinson started laughing.

'Ah, Jesus,' he said. 'Take a look at yourself!'

Some of the other lads were laughing too, sitting up in their beds.

Scottie wiped the layer of dust away from the mirror with his sleeve. His face and forehead were covered in thick dust, all except where his goggles had been.

'Like one of those bears in the zoo,' said Atkinson.

'Polar bear,' said McDonald.

'Polar bear's the arctic. It's white.'

'You mean a panda bear,' said a voice.

'No, polar bear, when its face is all bloody. I saw it on one of those documentaries.'

Scottie splashed some of the water from the bowl under the mirror on to his face while the lads turned to McDonald and started on him about his polar bear, then he dropped on to his bed and left them to it.

By midnight the storm had moved away. Scottie lay in the darkness, toying with the St Christopher Mel had given him, thinking of home. Lads were snoring on all sides of him. Every few seconds one of them had to cough away the sand and dust from their throats. The coughing rebounded from one side of the room to the other and back again. Scottie turned over in his bed, pressed his nose towards the wall, pulled his sleeping bag over his head and tried to escape again. But there was no escape. The more he tried to ignore the coughing the more awake he became. In the end he sat up, grabbed his penlight, switched it on and took a sip of water from his bottle. He checked how much water was left, fumbled around in the pouch of his bag until he found the last letter he'd got from Mel. It was nearly three weeks old. He

read it once, twice, again and again, analysed each word for all
of its possible meanings so that the letter took on a different
life each time he read it and then he started writing a letter
back to her, telling her how he was ready to come home
already, how he was counting the days, where he was going to
take her when he got back, what they were going to do
together. He wrote six pages then read them back in the
torchlight. He stuck the pages in an envelope and wrote her
name and address on the front, imagined her finding the letter
on the doormat, thought about how the next set of fingers to
touch the pages inside would be hers. But it didn't make him
feel okay. He started thinking about the days before he left and
the things he'd said to her, the things she'd said, the way she'd
reacted and that caused him to start imagining things, somebody else reading his words, laughing, Mel chucking the letter in a drawer and forgetting about it. In the end he stuffed
the envelope deep into his pack, switched off the torch and
rested his head back, feeling the tension drain from his neck
and shoulders. He concentrated on not concentrating but now
he wasn't tired enough to sleep. Writing the letter got him
thinking about the other letter he'd been meaning to write,
the one he'd seen a lot of the lads writing. It wasn't meant for
anybody except if something happened, something final. He
switched the torch back on and started writing his own. He
wrote it to his mam and said goodbye in it, told her how sorry
he was for letting something happen. He told her not to be sad
and that he was proud to have done a job that meant something, making sure there was nothing that would upset her or
get her thinking he regretted joining the army, making sure
there was no way on earth she could blame herself or anyone
else. He signed it to his sister and wrote a special note to her
underneath, telling her to look after their mam and to be
strong. He felt weird writing it but once he'd started he
couldn't stop. He wrote one for Drew and Mackie too, stuck
those letters in the same envelope. He got sick of what he was

doing after that and started thinking about it too much. In the end he stopped, forced them all in one envelope and put them in his bag with Mel's letter. Then for the third time he tried getting some sleep.

It was too hot though. He hated not having any air to breathe. When he couldn't stand it any longer he climbed on to the roof where the air was breathable. There was an unusual shape up there and a voice came out of the darkness.

'You too?'

It was Atkinson.

'How long have you been doing this?' Scottie asked.

'Since the second week,' said Atkinson.

'And nobody's said anything?'

Atkinson looked past Scottie into the night.

'Look over there,' he said.

Scottie turned and looked back across the roofs. He could see them in the shadows, dark figures scattered here and there, some smoking, the cigarettes glowing in the darkness.

'Jesus,' said Scottie.

'They don't train you for this,' said Atkinson.

'No,' said Scottie. 'Jesus Christ.'

Atkinson took another drag on his cigarette.

'And you're not bothered about mortars?'

'What's to be bothered about? We're as safe here as anywhere. Besides, you just hop off the side. Quicker than the door.'

'I suppose,' said Scottie. He peered over the edge to see where the ground was but there was just blackness there, nothing to see.

'You remember your birthday paintball treat?' Atkinson asked him.

'I'm hardly likely to forget,' said Scottie.

'You didn't enjoy it, did you?'

Scottie shook his head.

'I'm not into all that crap,' said Scottie. 'I don't like big groups and I don't like having to be up for a laugh every minute of every day like some of the lads.'

'What were you doing before?'

'Before what?'

'Before you came up. I saw your torch.'

'I was writing a letter,' said Scottie. Then he added, 'The one just in case. I was writing that.'

Atkinson lit another cigarette.

'Have you written one?' Scottie asked.

Atkinson shook his head.

'Why not?'

'It's just not my thing,' said Atkinson.

'It's not my thing either,' said Scottie.

'So why are you writing one?'

'I don't know,' he said. 'Because all the other lads have, I suppose.'

Atkinson stubbed his cigarette out and looked hard at Scottie in the darkness.

'But you're not like them,' he said. 'You're officer material. All the lads know it. All the officers know it too.'

'You're joking,' said Scottie.

Atkinson shook his head.

'You're a natural,' he said. 'You don't have anything to prove. They're a good bunch of lads but they'll always be a bunch of lads. You're an individual. They look to you. Like those days on the range and the day Miller disappeared.'

'I thought you were the one they looked to,' said Scottie.

'Aye, they do,' said Atkinson. 'They expect me to have all the ideas but once you said we should go back it was you they followed.'

'Well, I reckon you're the officer, mate,' said Scottie. 'Not me.'

Atkinson shrugged.

'Maybe I am,' he said. 'But you are too. Mark my words.

You shouldn't be writing letters like that. You shouldn't even be thinking about that sort of thing.'

'How can you not think of that sort of thing?' asked Scottie. 'In this place?'

What Atkinson had said about being an officer didn't bother him that much. He wasn't interested. But Atkinson might have been right about the letter. Maybe it was better not to think about it and to stay positive. Maybe thinking about it could cause it to happen. All he wanted to do was go home to Mel, sit her down and plan another way for the both of them and find out why it was that he hadn't heard from her in three whole weeks. He hoped it was just the post. Sometimes it was like that.

'You got anyone at home?' he asked Atkinson.

Atkinson shook his head.

'Not at the minute,' he said. 'Once I knew I was signing up I couldn't see the point. I know you have though.'

'Aye,' said Scottie. 'I have.'

Then, after a while of staring out over the rooftops he said, 'Do you ever wonder what we're doing here?'

'All the time,' said Atkinson.

'Me too,' said Scottie.

'Why, do you reckon?' Atkinson asked.

'I don't know.'

Atkinson shook his head.

'Me neither.'

'I'll tell you something though,' said Scottie. 'Back at home there's me and my mates, Drew and Mackie. You'd fit right in. You're the most like them. Well, you're the most like Drew anyway. You're not like Mackie. Nobody is. And he's not at home now anyway.'

'Why, what's he doing?'

'Working in a bar in Portugal. Getting knocked back by a different bird every night I expect. Drew's still home. He tried to sign up when I did but he failed the medical.'

'Jammy bastard,' said Atkinson.

'Aye,' said Scottie. 'He was gutted about it, too. Can you believe it?'

Full of scoff one morning, Scottie took himself on a few laps of the camp. An engineer caught him eyeing up the helicopters as he passed them and Scottie stopped to speak to him.

'You can forget about these,' said the engineer. They're not going anywhere.'

'What's wrong with them?'

'It's the sand. It's eaten up the rotor blades. We've got this to make it better.'

He pulled out a roll of tape from the box at his feet.

'What do you think? A multimillion pound piece of kit and we're patching it up with this stuff.'

Scottie laughed.

'Have your boys got all they need?'

'Most of it,' said Scottie. 'They reckon the ECMs for the Land Rovers are coming any day.'

The guy laughed.

'Where have I heard that one before?' he said.

A breeze came up and shot a load of sand into Scottie's face. Scottie coughed.

'Get used to it. You'll be here a while.'

'Six months,' said Scottie.

'Six months this time,' said the soldier. 'Then again and again . . . .'

'You reckon?' asked Scottie.

'Yep. And if not here somewhere else. This is going to run and run. Not for me, though. After this one I'm through.'

'How long have you been in?'

'Sixteen years. You?'

'About sixteen weeks,' he said.

The soldier laughed, but it was laughter with strings attached.

Scottie carried on walking, taking it all in. Men were sat in the shadows of the makeshift buildings, hiding from the heat. They looked at him like he was mad just for being out in it. He thought about writing the letter. He knew his mam would hate to think he'd written a letter like that. It wouldn't just upset her, it would crush her. It was better to just say everything was okay, that he was safe and there was nothing for her to worry about except organising his coming home bash at The Thistle. So he couldn't send it, couldn't let her have it sitting there on the mantelpiece at home forever reminding her of what might happen. But then if it happened there'd be no chance of a last goodbye, unless he put it somewhere, kept it on him. He'd be leaving to chance that they'd find it and send it on, but they might, if he put it in the right place. It was something he was going to have to decide on.

35

There were no letters from Mel. They stopped very abruptly whilst the other lads continued to receive theirs so he knew something wasn't right. He tried calling her but it was a battle to get any time on the phones and he missed her at home three times in a row. He started to get frantic about it but on the fourth time she answered and she seemed fine. She told him a letter was on its way but the letter didn't come.

He visited the gym whenever he got a free moment, to get the business with Mel off his mind and to defeat the boredom, lifting weights, doing push-ups, sit-ups, the works. His biceps and chest were cut better than they'd ever been, a combination of the weights and the sweaty heat draining the fat off. He hardly recognised himself whenever he got sight of a mirror. His skin was tanned bronze, his hair blond, bleached by the sun. When he had time off and when he could stand the heat he got himself up on the roof to top up his tan. The lads called it 'tan ops'. They weren't supposed to sunbathe on the roofs and they weren't meant to sleep on the roofs either but as the weeks turned into months more and more of the lads started until in the end they were just left to get on with it. Rockets or mortars. It didn't make much difference. When one came at the base it was just a case of dashing for cover and hoping. A lad could get caught outside a dozen times and not get a scratch, while another could do everything by the book and receive a direct hit. It was a lottery, down to chance, winners and losers. Looking at it any other way could drive you insane.

Bit by bit the lads adjusted to their surroundings, the ringleaders always searching out new ways to pass the time and kill the boredom. One of the senior lads delayed his wedding when he was posted and when the date came around the lads staged a mock wedding by marrying him off to McHugh. Atkinson's mam sent her old wedding dress out for the purpose. They wanted Scottie to play the bride but when the dress arrived Scottie didn't have a hope in hell of fitting it so they made McHugh do it instead. They fitted him up with the works, stockings, garter, high heels, and staged the whole ceremony from beginning to end. It was an excuse for a party, even one without drink, and it kept their minds off the serious business that faced them each and every day. It kept his mind off Mel too, the whole crap business.

Security patrol after security patrol came and went, the lads moving out into the surrounding countryside, making their presence felt. Nothing much happened on any of them. Each town was the same, life going on as normal but always the threat of something. Scottie had to use all of his powers of concentration to get through them and always ended up feeling knackered and drained before the squad leader called them in. Then it was back to the truck, the lads climbing aboard, watching their backs until the dust from the wheels hid everything from view, then the ride to base, never knowing when something might happen, whether a roadside bomb was waiting for them, lurking in a gutter somewhere. There wasn't enough body armour to go around and that played on his mind sometimes. Most of the lads only had one plate instead of two so they made use of it the best they could by strapping it across their chests. Scottie hated the thing anyway. He moaned about it every morning.

'It's hot enough without strapping this on.'

'You won't be complaining if a lump of shrapnel comes flying your way,' said Atkinson.

'No, I'll be too busy ducking,' Scottie said.

But he strapped the thing on all the same, thinking luck would decide if a chunk of metal was to hit him in that exact place and not somewhere else.

One morning the Warriors pulled out of camp with the lads inside, followed the highway for a time, a single carriageway road, straight as a runway through featureless desert. There were no buildings, just the pockmarked road. Sometimes the wheels would run over a hole and the Warrior would bounce on its suspension. Scottie was knocked about in his seat, knocked against Colton's shoulder, knocked against Atkinson. He gripped the strap above him in an effort to steady himself.

Every now and then the Warriors stopped. The lads spoke quietly to one another, aware that whenever they were not moving they were sitting ducks to whatever might be thrown at them.

'Your Hoops lost on Saturday,' said McDonald, grinning. He hated the Hoops as much as Scottie loved them.

'They didn't,' Scottie answered.

'They did too,' said McDonald. 'It was on the radio.'

'You're talking rubbish,' said Scottie.

McDonald looked at him and grinned.

'See,' said Scottie. 'I knew you were talking rubbish. What do you know about football?'

They started off again, passed a clump of flat-roofed farmhouses. There were chickens running around at the roadside. McDonald raised his rifle and took aim at one.

'Bang,' he said. 'Who wants roast chicken for scoff tonight?'

'Them,' said Atkinson. 'They're all skin and bone. It wouldn't be worth it. Anyway, shooting it with that there'd be nothing left of the thing.'

An old woman in black robes appeared. She stared after them. When Atkinson waved she grinned a toothless grin.

'One happy customer,' said Atkinson.

'Just your type,' said McDonald.

Minutes passed before they pulled up again. There they sat, the heat rising, sweat building. After a while, after the all-clear, they were ordered to disembark and set down. There was a palm grove at the side of the road and they headed for the shelter of the trees. Next to the palm grove was a rusting shell of a tank, one left over from a war long since ended. McDonald took a disposable camera out of his pack and got them all to line up in front of it. The lads did as they were told, crowding around the thing, clambering on to what was left of the turret, pushing their chests out.

'I'll tell me mam we captured it,' he said. 'She'll never know!'

Just then two kids came up the road from the flat-roofed houses where the chickens were roaming. They were no older than nine or ten but when they saw the soldiers on the tank they started shouting in high-pitched voices, pointing and waving their arms. The lads carried on regardless, even when the kids sandwiched McDonald and started grabbing at his camera. McDonald waved them off and shouted at them but they ignored him. Some of the lads started laughing.

'Hey, McDonald. Wait till your mam sees this! Is that the tank crew you captured?'

'It doesn't matter,' he said. 'I got a good one before they came.'

The children carried on shouting, pushing and pulling at the lads, pointing at the ground.

'They want us off,' said Scottie.

'I think we're playing on their climbing frame,' said Atkinson.

As soon as the lads moved, one of the kids clambered on to the cannon and straddled it, legs dangling, then he twisted himself around until he was hanging upside down.

'Take a photo with the kids in,' said Scottie. 'My mam'll love that even more. It'll stop her worrying.'

Scottie went and stood next to the smaller kid and posed for a photo. Now that the kids had the tank back they didn't seem too worried about the soldiers. The lads dug through their pockets for sweets and shared them with the kids until the kids stopped worrying about the lads stealing their tank and all was well in the world.

Time stopped while they waited for the order to move on. It was mid-morning and the haze had lifted. Some of the lads found shade under the trees, others propped themselves up against the tank, their backs against the rusted metal. Scottie was one of them. He closed his eyes and shut out the daylight. He was learning about waiting. It should have been one of the first questions they asked in the interviews.

'How good are you at waiting in one place? How good are you at doing nothing at all?'

After a while the sun was directly above them and there was no protection from it anywhere. McDonald crawled underneath the tank to show he knew differently.

'Hey, it's almost cool under here,' he said.

Seconds later he started screaming in pain. The lads jumped to their feet. He crawled out of the darkness holding his left hand.

'What is it?' shouted Scottie.

'Something bit me. A snake. I think it was a snake!'

'It wasn't a bite. It was a sting. A scorpion. A black one. I saw it run under the track.'

'It's a Death Stalker!' shouted McDonald. He was turning white in the face.

'It's not a Death Stalker.'

'It is! I know it.' He started rolling around in the dry earth.

'A minute ago you thought it was a snake. Just stay calm. It wasn't a Death Stalker. How do you feel?'

'It hurts. It's spreading.'

The two kids jumped down from the tank. They stood watching McDonald as he rolled around on the ground in the dust, until his uniform was caked in it. Then the smallest one cried out and ducked underneath the tank. He came out seconds later with the scorpion in his hand. The older one ran to his side and the two of them set off back towards the farm buildings with their find.

Atkinson looked down at McDonald.

'I think you just met the family pet,' he said. 'You just need to put some ice on it.'

'That's a good one! Yeah. I'll just put some ice on it.'

He pointed to the desert.

'We'd better get him to a medic,' he said. 'Just in case.'

McDonald's hand was reddening where the scorpion had stung him. He was clutching his wrist, complaining that the pain was travelling up his arm. Atkinson took him to the Warriors. When he came back five minutes later he was sweating from every pore.

'They're sorting him. We're moving in ten minutes,' said Atkinson.

'They said that an hour ago,' said Scottie but he picked himself up and set off back anyway. He had an idea that the inside of the Land Rover might be cool somehow but when he got there he realised that had been a fantasy. Instead the inside was like an oven and it would be like that until they got going, then maybe, if they were lucky, they'd get some sort of breeze flowing through, some sort of relief.

Another hour passed and they still didn't move. McDonald came back.

'It wasn't a Death Stalker,' he said.

The lads thought he was hilarious.

'You wait until it happens to you,' he said.

'I won't be crawling under any tanks,' said Atkinson. 'Weren't you listening in briefing?'

McDonald shook his head and went back to nursing his arm.

'I must have missed that one,' he said. 'Jesus, give me an old-fashioned wasp sting any day of the week!'

Artillery fire came in over the marshes, one explosion and then another while the lads kept their heads down and watched the spectacle. There was the puff and billowing of grey cloud as the shells landed and then the booming sound rolled across the valley to their ears. A herd of goats bolted from the source of the first, only to be caught up in the second. Those that made it through tore a path towards the water and were lost in the reeds. Shouts and cheers went out from the lads up the road. Scottie watched from his position, watched the smoke and dust rise up from the earth and slowly swallow the redness of the desert. Nothing else happened. Nothing emerged from within it. Nothing moved except the goats down by the reeds. One was limping badly, dragging its hind quarters behind itself. Scottie watched it until it collapsed pathetically to the floor. He waited for the all-clear and when it came he got to his feet and they started towards the scene of the explosions to see what was left behind.

The buildings were squat and ramshackle, some hardly buildings at all. Smoke was rising from behind a cluster and as the lads turned the corner the full extent of the destruction revealed itself. The building directly behind the first was now nothing more than a pile of smoking rubble. Close by, a palm tree had been torn and ripped from the scorched and blackened earth. Two dead goats were lying in the dirt, one with its neck twisted back on itself. There were piles of scattered rags, something white, something red, something torn and useless.

An old woman appeared out of nowhere. She was dressed in black and had a crooked spine. She came towards the lads with her hands at her ears, shouting, shouting, shouting. The lads retreated in small backward steps as she came upon them.

Only the interpreter stepped forward, the two of them both shouting now in the language they understood, the lads watching, clueless. Now from somewhere else an ageing man emerged. He had hands like blackened leather. He joined the shouting. Soon the CO was shouting too, trying to drown out the others.

'What are they shouting? What are they shouting?'

'Blood for blood,' said the interpreter. 'They are shouting blood for blood.'

'Well, tell them to shut it or we'll take them in. I don't want to listen to that kind of crap.'

Other faces appeared from the buildings, women, children, older boys, some men too, looking weak and pathetic, terrified, without hope, defeated by things that were beyond them. Scottie stared at their faces, his finger resting on the trigger, his dry tongue resting in his dry mouth, his eyes resting on one set of eyes and then moving on to the next, not knowing anything, not feeling anything, just watching, keeping alert, staying with it all.

They found four dead men in the rubble of the building and enough weaponry to cause a real mess. But they found two more bodies in the field beyond and it was these that had the old couple in such a state. Scottie wondered if they were related, if they were sons or grandsons, nephews, family. He watched the officers as they did their best to deal with the situation, thinking about how it was impossible to fight a war against an enemy you couldn't identify, how it made a mockery of all of the training and preparation he'd been through.

Waiting for the signal to move on and complete their patrol, Atkinson caught Scottie alone. He collapsed down next to him in the dirt and lit up a smoke.

'I was thinking about your question,' he said. 'The one about why I'm here.'

'Don't tell me, for Queen and country.'

Atkinson shook his head.

'Not for the money.'

Atkinson laughed.

'Now you're taking the piss.'

'What then?'

'You know already. I do it for the same reasons as you.'

'Go on then,' said Scottie. 'Amaze me.'

'For the lads. For each other. For all of us. What other reason is there?'

'So you don't let them down?'

Atkinson nodded quietly.

'Exactly that,' he said. 'It's why ninety per cent of us are here and why we didn't do a runner at the first sign they were sending us out.'

''Cause we're in it together,' said Scottie. 'That's what I told Mel.'

'She didn't want you to go?'

'Only at the end. She was all right before. It's not her fault. Anyway, it was this or plucking feathers off chickens and standing in a fridge all day.'

Atkinson laughed.

'Did you finish that letter?'

'Aye,' said Scottie. 'I wrote three in the end.'

'You believe there's something after all of this, then?'

Scottie shrugged.

'Not really,' he said. 'Mel's mam, she believes in all that. I suppose I think about it sometimes. That's got nothing to do with the letters though.'

'Of course it has. You're saying stuff after it's happened.'

'Only goodbye, stuff like that.'

Atkinson laughed again.

'Not we'll meet again? I'll bet you did. I bet you wrote "We'll meet again."'

Scottie laughed back.

'If this is the last place I see there'd better be something else,' he said. 'I mean, just look at it. What are we doing here?'

36

Another dawn brought another patrol. Scottie's unit left the base under a blanket of stars, taking advantage of the relative coolness, trying to get the job done before the sun became too stifling. They headed out in the Snatches, one following the other at distance, out of the gates of the compound, across the desert, an empty road, passing the dark outlines of squat, flat-roofed buildings, concrete barricades separating one carriage-way from the other, the drone of the vehicles threatening to drag the lads back into sleep, only the coughing, the endless coughing, and their adrenalin keeping them awake. On they went into the silent city. Scottie watched from the back of the Snatch, thinking of home and the night he left it, thinking of dates and numbers, how long he'd been on tour, how long he had to go, thinking of Mel, worrying and then convincing himself it would all be okay, turning himself in circles, imagining the comfort and warmth of a shared bed, fish and chips, lager, the Hoops, imagining arguments, break-ups, reconciliations. It was too early for chit-chat. The lads had fallen into themselves, each one making his own trip home, revisiting his own places, combating his own silent fears.

They disembarked in the financial district under the first orange flames of morning and set off on foot, spread out at intervals on both sides of the street, the vehicles between them, each soldier moving carefully, cautiously, communicating in hand signals, lads ahead and behind, checking doorways and alleyways, shadows and dark corners, alert to the slightest irregularity. It was just like their training in every possible way except that it was for real.

For a long while there was nothing, just the dawn, the orange light spreading, the lads moving up one street and down the next, looking to flush out trouble, hoping not to discover any. But trouble came anyway in the form of scuttling figures in the shrouds of darkness ahead. There were nine or ten of them, maybe more, scurrying in hunched posture across the street, some carrying objects at their hip, some above their heads, some carrying things in pairs, in threes and fours, moving from one side of the road to the other. For a moment time stood still. Scottie saw two men race across the road, furtively, like ghosts. He had just enough time to think of the midnight foxes he sometimes met when he was on his way back from The Thistle.

Rifle fire, shouting, confusion, chaos. In the half-light Scottie couldn't see who was firing where. He just got himself into the nearest doorway, dropped to position and pointed his rifle at where the action was playing out. More figures and forms appeared, running in all directions now, in the road ahead or standing motionless with their arms raised, some doing one thing and then the other, everything switching and changing impossibly. Bewildered by it all, watching the lads around him fire their weapons, Scottie did the same. Up ahead of him, in his very line of fire, one of the shadow men fell to the ground.

As soon as it had begun it was over. The firing stopped. The street was empty except for some scattered electrical goods and the downed man. He was shouting and screaming, his voice the only sound in the morning, the focus of everything. Nobody went to help him. The lads kept themselves under cover, waiting for the order to move. Throughout the time that passed while Scottie and the others waited, the man in the road lay shouting, his voice rising upwards between the buildings, a desperate, helpless sound. From somewhere far away, a dog started barking back at it.

Too many minutes later the lads were ordered to move on. Scottie passed the man in the street as the medics got to him. He was curled up on the concrete, his hands pressed against his stomach, a smashed portable TV lying in the road by his side, the oldest model, the sort his mam and Terry kept in the attic. The man's eyes were wide and staring. Scottie saw the whiteness there, the blood on the clothing and fingers, knew he was looking at a dying man, slithers of morning providing the backdrop to the scene.

The numbness, something that would threaten to overcome him in the days that followed, started its relentless creeping through Scottie at that very moment. There was no denying it once it found him. The image of the man in the road remained vivid and immediate. He couldn't stop thinking about the time between firing his weapon and the man collapsing in the road, couldn't get the idea out of his head that he was the one who had put the man there. It didn't matter about the confusion of the events or that some of the other lads were feeling the same because none of them talked about it, as he himself could not talk about it, and each time he convinced himself he wasn't the one another part of him repeated the suggestion that he was. No training anywhere, no amount of planning, no wise words or arguments could prepare a person for that.

He was eighteen years old and he had killed another human being. His Uncle Jack had been right. He had this image of the moment in his head, the man standing in the street, the TV in his arms, his eyes fixed right on Scottie's at the very moment that Scottie squeezed the trigger, a look that begged Scottie not to do it even as he did, the eyes widening, no distance between them at all, no half-light of morning, no confusion, his face right there, everything in faultless, resounding, indelible clarity, forever.

37

Out of the blue he got a letter from Mel. After weeks of waiting there it was, just like that, sitting in his palms. He took it back to his bed and prepared himself for opening it, getting all the little jobs out of the way first so he could concentrate on it properly. He was nervous in his stomach about it, his head full of stupid ideas.

He was all set to read it when the shout came up. They were heading out again. He shoved the letter into his bag, saving it for later. It was something to look forward to. He geared himself up and went to join the others.

It was a hot day, one of the hottest they'd faced. Each time Scottie thought he was getting used to the heat the sun would take things up a notch. Sometimes it felt like that was how the tour was going, up a notch, up a notch, things tightening and squeezing, then there'd be a day of doing nothing followed by another day just like that and it would feel like everything was slowing to a halt. It was difficult to know how to play it, what state to be in.

Same as every other day they followed the dusty road out of the camp, their Snatch third in line, Scottie, Atkinson and McDonald in the back, Colton riding up top, uneasy silence occasionally broken by jokes and banter, the silence returning.

They came over a little rise in the road and ran straight into gunfire. It came out of the desert, out of nowhere, harsh cracks and strange zips of sound. The lads clambered out of the vehicle, Scottie third in line, boots hitting the packed earth, knees bending on impact, rolling and moving, sprinting hard left through the dust clouds to the road edge, dropping to the ground, getting out of sight, the whizz and whine of more bullets screaming overhead. Scottie flattened himself against the ground. Above him Colton was already firing shots off from the top of the ditch, firing through the dust, burst after burst. The rest of the lads were spread out along the edge of the road, below the sight line of the enemy. More bullets zipped over them. Scottie kept his head down and waited, thinking that it was happening again, the image of the man in the road pressing for his attention. He stayed with his face in the dirt, fought to make himself smaller than he was, scrunching his knees up tight to his chest, hugging his rifle until the firing abated. When he got his head up the two officers were peeking and pointing above the parapet of the road. He stayed put until the officers grew more brazen and then he lifted his eyes and crawled up to join them, just far enough to see.

There was a building beyond the field, a storage facility of some kind and from the way the officers were pointing the gunmen were inside it. The lads brought the machine gun forward and set it up, then they started spraying bullets at the building. Mortar and cement disintegrated and the structure started to crumble. Dust exploded over the landscape, engulfing it. This was how they spent the next hour, firing bursts at the building between clouds of dust until there was nothing left of the building at all. After that they waited. Then they waited some more. Nobody fired back at them.

They got back into the Snatch and moved on again towards the village, the lads checking their rifles in silence, checking themselves, dusting their uniforms down, Scottie refusing to let the image of the man in the street work its way into him. To fight it he turned to Atkinson. The two of them caught each other's expressions and started laughing, nervous laughter that was infectious. It travelled easily between the lads, each one catching it. Soon they were carrying on where they'd left off, most of them hyped up now, talking their way through it all, the fizz of enemy fire, the way the building had crumbled to dust, how Colton had reacted so quickly, how the rest of them hadn't.

A nanosecond later the world exploded. White heat and deafening sound engulfed them. All Scottie knew was the sky above him, the feeling of being flung through the air, hitting the ground, rolling, the impact blurring everything. Lying in the dust, his ears ringing, he caught sight of a twisted shape beside him, a crumpled uniform, red fire, black smoke, a broken and bent rifle in the sand, a sound that might or might not have been human.

And screaming.

Screaming.

Screaming for a mother.

Fighting to stay with it, his senses numbed, Scottie instinctively searched for cover. There was a building to the right, no more than fifty metres away. Colton appeared beside him. The two of them shared a nod and then they were on their feet and running, running together through the chaos. For a moment they were back on the selection weekend, back on a muddy field, Colton's white trainers sparkling, drizzle cooling their faces, their lungs full of the fresh air of home.

Then there was another explosion.

Part Three

38

Scottie woke in a room with a white ceiling. The walls were white too, the paint flaking and peeling, windows broken, the floor covered in shattered glass, a sliver of blue beyond them and a defined shade where the light came through and where it couldn't penetrate. He was propped up against a wall in the shade. The wall was cool on his back but he was sweating despite it, sweating from every pore.

Footsteps sounded in the corridor beyond the door. One of the lads ran past without looking in on him. There was the crack of more gunfire, a moment of silence then more shots, shouting, a mess of confused voices.

He was in a schoolroom. There were no desks but there were other things. There was a blackboard fixed to the wall, some writing on it, a smeared trail of blood on the floor, leading in from the door, leading to the place where he was sitting. A cold dread ran through him. There was too much blood. Beside him on the floor was his body armour. It was smeared with blood. He tried to reach out for it but as soon as he did the pain became too much to bear, came in waves so fierce he could hardly stay with it.

He looked upward, tried to fight the feeling washing over him. There were children's paintings stuck to the wall, pictures of houses and families, brothers and sisters, shapes and figures. He tried to concentrate on them but it was impossible.

There was something wrong with his right shoulder. He forced his eyes toward it. He couldn't tell what was his uniform and what was his own charred flesh. He vomited. All he could smell was that and the cordite from the weapons.

In the next second the room was filled with deafening sound. The walls of the classroom shook all around him. Dust came down from the ceiling and rose up from the floor. Dust came in through the window, swirled in the air. He was engulfed by it and it carried him to places and people . . .

. . . his mother

. . . his sister

. . . his friends

. . . his places

. . . pictures that flexed and changed. He saw his mam get off the bus on Hillside, heading back from the shops, saw her stop in the street and set her bags down, saw her turn her head as if looking for something she was expecting to be there, saw the puzzled expression on her face when nothing came.

He saw Drew in the little office at the back of the school buildings, saw him sitting there, a mug of tea steaming on the workbench, Drew staring straight through it, miles away, thinking about something, getting a feeling.

He saw Mackie splayed out topless in a dark room, bright sunlight forcing its way between the slats in the shutters, music thumping beyond the walls, sweat gathering in the small of his back, a fan humming, saw Mackie wake with a start and turn over to stare at the ceiling, his eyes red with lack of sleep.

He saw Mel staring at the mirror in the hairdresser's, freeze in a position, stare at herself while the woman in the chair tilted her head back to look at her in puzzlement.

He saw all of these things, felt them, lived them, each picture forming and then dissolving, edges melting to nothing, red fog descending, altering, becoming sand, becoming dust, everything turning to dust, all the world shrouded in a thick layer of dust. He was buried in it. It choked him, weighed him down. He couldn't move for it. All he knew was the white heat of the wound in his shoulder and the white heat of the village, the buildings trapping the heat between them, the darkness of shadows behind windows and doorways.

He could sense only some of it, the way the stretcher lurched as they carried him towards the helicopter, the sand flying in all directions, rotor blades whirring, the noise of the machine, a giant shrieking bird, the men shouting above the sound, the pop and crackle of gunfire, distant now, somewhere else. And then he was rising upwards, away from the place, rising up and up and up.

The village shrunk away beneath him, became miniature. The dust retreated too. Turning his head to one side he could see the black smoke rising from the burned-out vehicles and buildings, faces close to his, busy hands, voices telling him to stay with it. They came and went in waves, were lost and found then lost again.

The helicopter followed the path of the river, meandering as the river meandered, a thin ribbon of life amongst the deadness of the desert; a dusty road running straight like a scar, sometimes alongside the river, sometimes losing it, but always the river returning to the road or the road returning to the river. And soon the river delta began to widen and within it the thin band of water widened too. They passed over a field of ploughed earth, a lonely scarecrow fixed in its centre. It was wearing a soldier's helmet, dressed in black. They passed over a shepherd herding goats. When he saw them he waved his crook at them. He looked like somebody from a children's bible. They'd had one at primary school and the teacher read from it each week, told them stories of shepherds and carpenters and Kings. And there on the road below was a man walking a donkey. These images rose and fell at will. He had no understanding of what was real and what was not. Primary school, a Christmas dinner, the school hall decked in Christmas decorations they'd all made, turkey and roast potatoes, on the wall a cardboard donkey and a man leading it. He could remember the words. 'Little Donkey, Little Donkey . . .'

They came easily to him.

The river was full and healthy now and the desert had lost its grip. Below him was the river basin, fields of green sprouting from the water on each bank, long-legged birds wading in the shallows. They turned their beaks towards the beast above and watched from amongst the bulrushes. In his head another picture from the Bible, the baby in the basket, his mother letting the basket be taken by the river, the look in her eyes, the bulrushes tall around both of them. And there was Moses too, in his basket floating through the bulrushes, a boy all alone.

Water buffalo heavy in the reeds, a magical field of sunflowers, the river silver and gold in the evening light, the marshlands spreading to the horizon. Scottie only caught tiny fragments, tiny splashes of light and colour before the dust descended again, a black cloak that buried him.

Each time he woke he found himself in a new place, always lying on his back, always a ceiling above him, a fan humming, faces peering into his, blinding white lights, distant voices. Sometimes they spoke his name but he was never really with them, was always somewhere else. He felt only one feeling and came to learn that the feeling was guilt. It overwhelmed him despite himself.

Most of the time he visited home, each experience more real than the one before, him always a bystander looking in on the lives he'd left behind, unable to be part of things.

He passed through the alley and by the houses that were all in a row, over the school playing fields with their battered goalposts and down the hill to the hairdresser's where Mel worked. He saw her come out with the other girls and he stayed with them until they split their separate ways at the crossroads. She started up the hill towards the tenements and he followed at a distance, the sky turning from grey to black, night replacing day. He followed her across the tenement car park and up the stairs, watched her open the front door and go straight to the cabinet where her mam stacked the mail, saw her face fall when she saw there was no letter.

He wanted to tell her that it was okay, but he could only watch.

'Was there anything, Mam?'

'No, love, nothing.'

She walked into the living room and slumped down on the sofa. For a minute or two just sitting there, staring at the TV, then she opened her bag and took out her mobile. She sat there texting. A minute later the phone rang.

'Hiya. No. Nothing for a week. I'm fed up. Are you lot going out tonight?'

When she put the phone down her mam started up.

'They'll come,' she said. 'You know how it is.'

'I just need to go out so I don't spend the whole night thinking about it.'

'With Kirsty?'

'Yeah, her and Danielle. All that crowd.'

'It'll do you good,' said her mam.

She went upstairs and he went after her. She started the water running in the bath, chucked in a load of soap crystals. When the bath was full he watched her undress and climb in to the water, watched her sink down into the bubbles until just her head was above them. She closed her eyes. He knew she was thinking about him. He could sense it, but she was thinking about other things too, about going out with the girls, about what she was going to wear, how many weeks it had been since she last went out.

She took her time getting ready, made a meal out of it all, blow-drying her hair, trying this top and that, music blaring out on her stereo, ages in front of the mirror with her make-up. When she was done he saw how beautiful she was.

Her taxi came. The cab was full of her perfume and the

cab driver said something about it. She laughed, said it was a special occasion. The girls were already in the bar. Scottie didn't trust them. They didn't stick with any lad for five minutes. He could feel himself tensing up. They were drinking already, downing shots. They had two lined up for her when she walked into the place. She wasn't a drinker, couldn't handle her drink. She was glassy-eyed after the second one. He could see it affecting her. He wanted to step in and take her home but he was not there. Instead he was thousands of miles away and even though he'd written her letters she didn't have all of them, didn't know what he was up to, where he was, how much he was missing her. Now she was out drinking with some of the girls from school, girls that were only interested in one thing. He knew she wasn't like that, but she was drinking more already, some sort of cocktail. The girls were laughing about the name of it. One of them started making a show of sucking on a straw and the rest of them cackled and slowly, slowly Mel melted into them, became one of them, no longer separate, no longer his special girl, but someone else instead. Some of the lads in the bar were drawn in by their antics, lads with trendy haircuts, lads that spent all their money on clothes and making themselves look good, lads that Mel had always said she hated but she wasn't hating them now, she was laughing and joking with them, sipping away at her cocktail, so naive and such easy prey. He couldn't hear what the lads were saying to her because of the music and the racket in the place but he didn't need to hear to see she was enjoying the attention. This was how it happened. This was the beginning of it. Some of the lads had their mobiles out already, hunting numbers, reeling them in. He saw Mel take out her phone and some lad in a cream shirt, a good-looking lad, leaning in as close as he dared to take her number. There was a photo of Scottie on the phone but it didn't seem to matter. She took no notice of it. He told himself sharing numbers didn't mean anything, that being out with the girls like this meant nothing. A few drinks could change a person but they changed back afterwards. In the morning she'd wake up and laugh at herself, think about the way she'd behaved. She'd leave the lad's number on her phone but if he called she'd put him off, tell him she had a bloke in the army. It was normal behaviour. He just wasn't used to seeing it, wasn't used to Mel doing it, even though blokes went into the hairdresser's all of the time. She was in love with him. He was her bloke. Everybody knew it.

But not these lads.

And he wasn't there.

When he woke it was almost dark outside and the girl was speaking.
'None of this is real,' she said.

He got up and went over to her, placed his mouth by her ear.
'Shut up,' he said.

'But you know it, don't you? You know this isn't real.'
'Of course it's real.'

'You're wrong,' she said.

He touched her cheek. It was cold. He felt the wetness of her tears.
'If it's not real, why are you scared?' he asked.

'I'm not scared,' she said.

'Why are you crying then?'
'Because I feel sorry for you.'

'Sorry for what?'
'For what happened.'

'Nothing happened.'
'Do you really think that?' she asked.

'I told you to shut up,' he said. 'Just go to sleep. I'm not talking to you any more.'

He turned his back on her, moved over to the window. The sun was setting, red folds behind black cloud. It reminded him of the oil fires. It reminded him of the roadside bomb. She wouldn't shut up though. She kept on at him, asking the same question over and over until he crept back across the room, reached out, touched her cheek again.

'Can you feel that?'

'Yes,' she said.

'Exactly,' he said.

He squeezed harder and then stepped away from her, returned to the window, keeping his head low.

'That proves nothing,' she said.

He turned his back on her.

'I'm thirsty,' he said. 'That's the only thing I want to think about.'

'When's the last time you drank anything?' asked the girl.

He shrugged his shoulders.

'When's the last time you ate?'

'I can't remember,' he said. 'I can't remember anything, just the train and what happened last night outside the club. That's it.'

'What about the hospital? Did you eat there?'

He turned and looked at her blankly.

'I don't remember,' he said. 'I'd forgotten all about that place.'

39

Scottie was in a hospital bed. The next time he came out of it all he was in the same bed and so it went on until he understood himself to be somewhere permanent. Sunlight flooded the ward. Tiny flecks of dust danced in it. He let the light bathe his face, enjoying the warmth of it through the glass. There was a perfect blue sky beyond the window. He raised himself and twisted around to look out. There was a garden. It was sitting under a fine dusting of snow. The grass stems poking through the snow sparkled in the sunlight, each tiny blade distinctive from its neighbour. A blackbird landed on the grass and hopped through it, leaving tiny puffs of snow in its wake.

He spent hour on hour staring out of the window, watching the garden and examining the subtle changes that took place. There was nothing else to do. At times he felt like it was all he could cope with, to sit and stare out of the window, to have nothing else to think about but colours and shades. Whenever his mind drifted to more complicated things, it usually came up with questions. Why had he not seen a doctor that morning or why had he not heard from his mam and sister or Mel or Drew?

He slept most of the time, a lazy, drifting type of sleep that came in swirls like the snow sometimes did. It carried him to all sorts of places but settled him nowhere so that nothing became solid. Instead he only managed to catch fractured glimpses of things, the morning on the road in the Warrior, the stillness of the schoolroom while the world around it exploded, Tanner's Park, his house, his front door.

Sometimes he'd wake in the night and a cold terror would grip him as he thought about never leaving, being stuck forever waiting for his wounds to heal. Pain came in waves, subsiding to almost nothing at one moment and then crippling him, doubling him up, leaving him gasping the next. It was always worse at night when the ward was dark. There was nothing to see beyond the window at those times, no respite.

40

One night he saw a man standing at the end of his bed. He was in the centre aisle, dressed in hospital robes, face ashen, eyes wide and staring at nothing. The man moved silently between the beds in the darkness, moving from one end of the ward to the other. Wires and tubes were trailing from his chest and arms. He shuffled along on the cold tiles, not lifting his bare feet, just inching forwards. Scottie watched him from his bed. He had the covers up to his chin and he pretended his eyes were closed so the man would not see him. But the man was not looking at him. He was staring fixedly at the little window in the door at the end of the ward. The light of the next corridor shone through it, creating a square of brightness. He moved slowly on until he reached the door, then he lifted a hand and pulled it open. The light of the corridor started to fill Scottie's end of the ward, beginning with a thin crack and then flooding in. Scottie had to close his eyes against it. By the time his eyes adjusted the man had disappeared into it.

But the door did not swing shut. It remained open instead, the light shining in from beyond, shining directly on to Scottie's bed, urging him to follow. He felt his legs begin to move under the covers, sat upright and twisted his body until he was on the edge of the bed, the light sending a warm feeling though the whole of his being. Without thinking about it, without going through the processes and functions necessary to do so, Scottie felt himself rise. He stepped on to the floor, felt the cold tiles on the soles of his feet, moved towards the light, hardly aware of himself. He felt as though a great weight had been lifted. His shoulder and chest seemed lighter as if his injuries had never happened and the door remained open, impossibly open throughout. He was three steps from passing through it when the image of home entered his head. Without warning a picture formed, a bright summer morning beyond the bedroom window, the smell of toast from the kitchen, his mam moving about, music playing in the shed, his sister singing in the bathroom, Drew's voice calling from outside.

The door to the ward swung shut and the light went out. In an instant he was back in his bed again, the same dull pain simmering inside of him. Conscious now, he climbed out of bed and moved to the chair, taking his blanket with him, wrapping himself up in it, cocooning himself within it for protection. The garden outside was bathed in pure moonlight. It reflected off the snow-frosted plants and flowers, the night perfectly clear, like it had been on so many nights in the desert. The man from the ward was out there, wires and tubes still trailing from his forearms and chest. He was sat on a snow-sprinkled bench in his robes, still bare-footed, upright with his hands on his lap, his knees together, not moving at all.

Scottie couldn't leave him to freeze to death in the garden. He had to get dressed and get out there but all he had was the white hospital gown he was wearing. It didn't matter. The patient next to him had a dressing gown. It was laid out on the chair beside him. Scottie pulled it on. He stole the man's slippers too, made his way down the aisle between the beds, heading for the double doors. The lights were on beyond the square window, just as they had been before, but the lights were not as bright this time. Scottie hesitated before pushing the doors open, remembering the feelings he'd had. But this wasn't the same. He knew exactly where he was and what he was doing. He was going to get the man back inside, before he froze to death.

Each new corridor seemed colder than the one before it. The cold set his shoulder off so that the pain began to hammer at him. Gasping from it, he had to stop and lean against the wall, the corridor stretching away to nowhere, a row of strip lights, pure white walls, the floor white, everything white. And there was nobody, not a soul, just him, no other signs of life. He wondered how he would ever get to the end of it.

But he didn't have to. The pain in his chest abated. It helped him to see things more clearly. The corridor shrank back to size. There were nurses and doctors, a reception area, a set of doors that swished open and closed. Scottie walked through them. Nobody tried to stop him. Nobody took any notice of him at all.

It was snowing outside, heavy flakes falling like downy feathers, settling on the parked cars. Scottie turned, followed the path around the outside of the hospital, heading to the garden, wondering what he was going to do when he found the man, wondering what he was going to say to him. The pathway traced its way around the edge of the hospital buildings, the snow falling more heavily as he went. It was hard for him to find direction. He got his head down, focused on his feet and the steps he was taking. He thought about how crazy he looked and how crazy the man had looked. He thought about the dust storms in the desert, trudging through them to get to the toilet block or the canteen, fighting a way back.

He couldn't see anything ahead of him when he reached the next corner, could not keep his eyes open for long enough to make out shapes of things or gain perspective. He started to feel the cold and felt the pain in his chest ratchet up a notch. He felt for the hospital wall with his left hand, found a drain-pipe and grabbed it. Pain burst inside him, causing him to double up. For the first time since they'd brought him in, he felt truly frightened. There was nobody to help him. He could die out here in the hospital grounds. They'd find him crunched up in a corner somewhere.

'The soldier who went to the desert and died in the snow.'

It was crazy.

A tunnel of white filled his vision, the world outside of it diminishing to nothing. There was an unnatural brightness and, ridiculously, warmth too. He felt the urge to let go of the wall, to wander into the light and not look back, to not even think about it. The wind was no longer shrieking but singing instead. The feeling of nausea left him, as did the pain. And he almost went with it, almost let himself be carried away, was already leaving the security of the wall when the image of the man in the garden came back to him, the man on the bench, wires trailing, bare feet turning blue with the cold, the look on his face, of being lost, of being left behind. Scottie would not leave him behind. There was something about the man's face, something familiar. Like his Uncle Jack. The man looked like his Uncle Jack.

He felt for the drainpipe and steadied himself.

Immediately the pain came again but Scottie had a fresh determination now. He got his feet moving, battling forward against the blizzard. He forced himself to the corner of the building, then the next, his eyes searching beyond the blanket of white for the garden.

Only he could not find it. He turned one more corner and found himself back where he had started, at the hospital entrance. Every part of him ached. He wanted to try again, to keep trying until he found the man, but he needed to get inside too, to warm himself through. He made a decision, to go back to the ward and the window, to look at the garden from there, to try and locate a landmark close to the hospital walls and then to search for the landmark when he felt ready. The double doors swished open and Scottie fell into the warmth of the hospital foyer, made his way along the white corridor to the ward, the corridor shorter now, the walls less white than before, the lights less bright. When he reached the ward he went straight to the window by his bed. He wiped the condensation and pressed his nose against the glass. The blizzard was still hard at it. He couldn't see much but it looked like there was a garden right there where it should be, right where he had been. The bench was empty.

Later, lying in bed staring at the ceiling, a moment from his previous life popped into his head. He was at the hospital visiting his uncle the day before he passed away.

'Have you seen the garden?' his uncle asked him.

Scottie looked across at the window. His uncle was staring at it. Beyond the glass was the next wing of the hospital, grey concrete and windows, some lights on behind the glass, some windows dark and empty. Scottie got up and walked over, looked down to the ground, expecting to see a garden down there, but there was nothing, just concrete paving, leaves and rubbish blown into piles, trapped there by the wind.

He didn't say anything. Instead he looked into his uncle's distant eyes and spoke a lie.

'I see it,' he said. 'Do you like it?'

'It's the most beautiful garden I've ever seen,' said his uncle. Then he turned away from the window and drew Scottie towards him.

'Promise your uncle something,' he said. 'Promise you'll have one for me at The Thistle when this is all over.'

'Aye,' said Scottie. 'I will.'

He never had, though, not properly anyway, not in the way his uncle had meant. The funeral didn't count because The Thistle had been crowded, full of strangers and he'd gone on holiday right after it. Then he'd gone to the war zone. War had brought him to this hospital bed. Sure, he'd been to The Thistle and played pool with Drew. He'd even gone down with Terry for a swift one but his uncle meant something else. He was talking about standing at the bar, not talking to anybody, just supping his pint and letting everything settle. That was how he'd have a drink for his uncle, quietly, in his own way, alone.

He had to go home now and do exactly that, for his uncle and his mam and all of the others, to make good on promises. If they couldn't get to him he'd have to go and find them.

'There's a garden,' she said. 'That's where we need to go.'

'Why?'

She looked at him.

'You really don't know, do you?'

Scottie glanced at the floor.

'I've seen your garden. I saw it from the hospital. It was outside the window. When I was back on my feet I went outside to find it. I walked around the whole building but it wasn't there. It didn't exist.'

She stared at him with blank eyes.

He stared back, deliberately, challenging her.

'There isn't a garden,' he said. 'There isn't anything at all. This is it. This is all there is. This stinking place. Nothing else.'

'You're wrong,' she said.

'Am I? You keep saying that but you don't do anything about it. You just sit there staring, like you know something but you're afraid to say it. Are you afraid of me? Is that it?'

She shook her head.

He took the photograph of the dead soldier out of his pocket and dropped it on the floor in front of her.

'Look at him,' he said. 'Look at his face. He's not in any garden. He took a dozen bullets in the chest and when he landed his face looked like that, exactly like that.'

He sighed.

'If you know something then you have to tell me, because this isn't right.'

He walked to the window and looked out of it.

'Where is everybody?'

Nothing was happening.

'Things haven't been right since the train, maybe before, maybe right back before the hospital, before the helicopter . . .'

His voice trailed off. He thumped the wall, causing her to flinch at the sound, but she didn't answer him.

41

Next morning his bags appeared at the end of his bed. There was no explanation for it. They just appeared. The letter from Mel was crumpled up in the place where he'd stuffed it. He ripped open the envelope and read its contents with quickening breath, nausea overtaking him, growing stronger as each word lead to the next until the letter became a staccato blur of individual words and part sentences.

. . . trying to think of how to say it . . . missing you so much . . . everybody acting like you don't really exist any more . . . nobody talking about you in the present tense . . . going out and hating it because you're not here . . . wanting to watch the news and being scared to watch it . . . started thinking . . . started asking myself questions . . . stuck in the house . . . asked myself if I still love you . . . had to think about it . . . was always automatic, not something I had to think about . . . came to an answer . . . I do still love you . . . will always love you . . . but . . . scared . . . thinking . . . rest of my life with you? . . . feel bad about telling you . . . honest . . . truthful . . . even if it hurts . . . too young for this . . . I don't know if I want to spend the rest of my life with you . . . want different things . . . changed . . . all last night crying . . . scared to post it . . . probably regret . . . best thing that ever happened to me . . . concentrate on your job . . .

There was more, so much more, pages and pages, but he couldn't read them. He was burning up inside. He got dressed, his legs weak and feeble, gripping the cold iron rail of the bed to steady himself, dizziness threatening to send him crashing to the ground. He walked out of the double doors into the blinding light of the corridor. He got some strength in his legs, passed through the entrance doors and out into the cold, not looking back, headed down the gravel pathway, through the black iron gates and up the hill into the town. The snow had frozen into a hard crust. His feet crunched through it each time he took a step. It made walking difficult. Sometimes he lost his balance and had to check himself. The sudden unexpected movements hurt his shoulder, caused the pain to well up inside of him, but he was past caring.

At the station he walked straight on to the platform and on to the train. Nobody tried to stop him. He got himself comfortable, finding the right position for his shoulder and then he sat back and watched from the window as the train moved out of the station. It hadn't been so long ago that he'd boarded the train after saying goodbye to Drew. Now he was going home, his body and mind on auto pilot, his thoughts fixed only on the things he was going to find there, and Mel.

The carriage was almost empty. There was just him and a young girl at the far end. She was hunched up on her seat, staring out of the window, taking no notice of him. He watched her until she looked back at him, then he turned to the window himself. He spent the first hour of the journey staring out of it, taking in the countryside, grateful of it in a way he'd never thought possible. Mackie was forever going on about how miserable it all was but on this day, at this moment, Scottie felt comforted by everything he was seeing. After the holiday, after the deployment, after the hospital bed, he was happy just to sit and look at it all and feel part of it. And so he watched the country slip by, the white fields in so many random shapes, the snow-topped hedgerows and stone walls separating one from the next, the trees, each with their own unique covering of snow, sometimes a group clumped together, sometimes a solitary tree standing all alone, the cottages and church steeples, slated roofs under dirty white sprinklings of snow. Sometimes a town, the train dissecting it, its innards exposed, station platforms flashing by, people sat on station benches, hunched against the cold, staring out of themselves, grey forms displaying no sign of life; grey factories too, steel and concrete, chimney stacks rising up in the distance, blocks of flats towering over everything. Scottie saw the beauty in all of it. He was not a stranger any more or an outsider. He knew how these places worked, what their function was, just as he knew his place amongst them. He had not known his place and function for the last few months, had sometimes been told it by the officers but never fully understood it. And even when he'd started to feel he might understand it, things had happened to throw him off kilter and land him back where he started. Like the looter.

Scottie closed his eyes, blocked out any thought of it, knowing it was the only chance he had. To think of it would destroy him. He let the rhythm of the train carry him away, got to thinking about Mel instead. That was no better. Breathing awkwardly, trying to contain himself, panic just a touch away, his best defence against it was to let the tiredness underlining all he was feeling get a grip.

He woke on the outskirts of the city. His city. He couldn't help smiling as the thought came to him. The train was busier now. Voices of fellow passengers drifted down the carriage to his ears. The dialect was familiar. His dialect. He sat himself up in his seat and watched from the window. It was all there as he'd left it; the golf courses first and then the two motorways marking the boundary, grey concrete structures covered in graffiti; the estates climbing back towards the hills, all grey;

football pitches, a dozen of them all in a row, snow covering the lot, run-down changing rooms at each end, empty now, waiting. How many times had he and Drew battled it out on those pitches? Sunday mornings, games on every pitch, so many colours from so many kits, the shouting and the whistles, the cheers when a goal went in, and when they were just kids, heading down to the fields on a day like this, kicking about in the snow, Drew diving in every direction, both of them loving it, heading home soaked to the skin, pushing their bikes, too tired to ride. The great gasometer towers appeared, complete with huge placards promoting the city's latest attraction, then the retail parks, packed to bursting; on and in to the old city, the grandness of the buildings there, the history that almost choked him up.

Each time he turned his gaze away from the window his eyes fell on the girl's. She held his gaze until he was the one who had to drop his eyes and look out of the window again. He wished she would stop because he was flying inside, drinking everything in and when he got home, after he'd seen Mel, he was going to drink a pint with Drew and tell him all about it, about how they were lucky to have rain and wind and snow and fields and how the grey concrete was the best colour in the world. Drew would think him mad but he didn't care because he knew he was right.

The feeling didn't last. As the train slowed, as the city swallowed it, the buildings closing in above the tracks, the sky darkening, so his mood darkened. The euphoria he'd been feeling seeped out of his skin and left him. What replaced it was something else, something cold and unnerving. When the train pulled in at the station and the passengers took off into the evening Scottie stayed in his seat, the weight of the moment forcing him down, preventing him from moving, denying him his need to get up and step out into the future. His future. He only managed to move when the train and platform were empty. With his chest and shoulder burning he got himself up and out on to the platform. It stretched away in front of him, one long, soulless parade of grey concrete, riddled with puddles of standing water and rubbish, cardboard coffee cups and crisp packets, the lights of the station reflecting back off the water and dirty slush piles. Scottie trudged through it all, his legs heavy, his chest straining, the cold running into him and through him. As he walked a crowd of people started up the platform to board the train for its outward journey. They buffeted past him as he made his way toward the gate. Nobody took any notice of him. The guards at the gate paid him no attention either. Nobody looked in his direction at all.

Outside the station he boarded a bus for home, the city full of people going about their business, shop windows full of Christmas gifts, lights shining in a million different colours, hung between the buildings, twinkling in the grey afternoon. He huddled deeper into his coat, the pain in his shoulder coming in spasms, his throat parched with thirst.

The bus crossed the great river, the water brown and soupy, swirling and rolling, threatening to burst its banks. All around him were familiar places and memories. They came rolling over him like the river rolled. Christmas tree lights blinked from house windows, red-nosed reindeers lit up gardens, snowmen in Hoops shirts and scarves stood on scrublands separating one block of flats from the next.

And all the time he looked at these things something was gnawing away at him, the fear that Mel no longer loved him, that he was not going to be able to change any of it, that it was all over except the shouting, the fear too that the city had not acknowledged his return, that nothing and nobody cared a damn that he was back, that nothing and nobody had missed him for a single second during the time he'd been away.

He only noticed the girl again as he stepped from the bus. She'd been seated at the back the whole journey. Now he saw her watching him from the rear window as he stood on the pavement halfway down Hillside. Her eyes trained on his, not wavering, some connection existing between them, the bus moving away towards the cemetery and on into the evening traffic. He almost went after her. She was the only one who seemed to be taking any interest in him. Too late. The bus disappeared in a pool of red light, leaving him in the shadows on Hillside, standing by the cemetery railings, the snow heaped in filthy grey piles against the stone walls of the place.

He made his way down the hill until he reached the cemetery gates. There was a bench there. He brushed the snow from it and sat down, pulled his jacket tight and watched the cars and people, sinking deep into himself whenever a stranger passed, watching the hairdresser's window, his heart skipping a beat when he recognised Mel beyond the glass. She was busy, closing the shift down, sweeping, checking till receipts, meticulous and concentrated as always. In a few moments he was going to knock her perfect, mechanical world way out of kilter and all the ideas he'd entertained that the moment was going to be special and magic between them had somehow vanished into the blackness behind the cemetery walls.

42

He watched Mel say goodbye to her workmates and cross the road through the traffic, waited at the gates of the cemetery until she passed.

'Mel!'

To begin with she carried on walking, not recognising his voice.

'Mel, it's me!'

This time she turned. He saw her pretty face. She tottered, had to reach out and grab the cemetery railings for support, shook her head, shifted her feet, searching for a stable position.

'It's me, Mel.'

'No way,' she said. 'No way.'

He smiled.

'They sent me back. Medical reasons.'

He pointed to his shoulder.

'Obviously,' he said, laughing.

She found her feet, straightened. Her face was flushed and she couldn't meet his gaze.

'This isn't right,' she said.

He laughed again.

'Why are you laughing? It isn't funny.'

'Of course it's funny. I'm here. Look. Look at me.'

He shoved his index finger into his own chest to show he was real but she backed away from him.

He was thinking what to say next when her mobile rang. She ignored it, stood looking at him instead, eyes wide open.

'Why don't you answer it?' he asked her. 'Is it him?'

She shook her head.

'Who? What?'

'It's him, isn't it?'

'Go away. Leave me alone.'

'Is it because of what I said?'

'What?'

'In the shed that night?'

'What are you talking about?'

He couldn't bring himself to say it.

'I didn't come looking for you,' he said instead. 'If that's what you think. It's just the cemetery. My uncle . . .'

'Just leave me alone,' she said again.

He tried smiling but she turned away from him, steady on her heels now. He followed her until the railings ended and then he stopped, frightened to go on.

'Who's on the phone?' he shouted.

She turned.

'You didn't call,' she said. 'I waited but you didn't bother. What was I meant to do?'

'I was thousands of miles away, in a war!'

'Yeah, well, there was that too. Every day not knowing. Hearing it on the radio. Seeing it on the TV. People asking all the time. "How is he? Have you heard from him? Is he all right? No news is good news." I'm too young for all that. I wasn't ready to be a widow. He was here and you were there . . .'

'Not any more,' he said.

'Well, it's too late now,' she said. 'I don't know why you had to go in the first place. It wasn't your war.'

'It's somebody's,' he said.

'Yeah? Well it's not yours.'

'I didn't get a choice,' he shouted.

'Scottie, you chose to join the army. You chose. Nobody made you. You could have stayed here. We could have been here together.'

'I came back though, didn't I? I'm here! Mel, wait!'

But she wouldn't wait.

'I came back for you!'

He shouted her name again, louder this time, but his voice was lost in the traffic. It must have been because she didn't even flinch when he called her. It was like he wasn't even there. He didn't chase after her. He was frightened of pushing things to their limits so he let her go. His throat was impossibly dry. He needed a drink, of water or anything else, thought about sinking a pint in The Thistle then chased the thought away. Things weren't turning out the way he'd expected so why would a visit to The Thistle be any different? Why wouldn't it just send more things flying at him that he had no understanding of?

He tried imagining going home but didn't feel prepared for it any more. The events in the hospital, the feeling at the station, the meeting with Mel, the look on her face, had knocked him out of his stride. He wandered aimlessly around the estate instead, stumbling upon familiar places and then struggling to remember a thing about them. He kept to the shadows, avoiding people's eyes when they passed him. Nobody recognised him. Pretty soon the snow came again, white flakes filling the darkness, falling with purpose, taking up residence on the ground, creating a carpet of white in front of him. He walked and walked, unsure of where the next step would take him, not even thinking about it, all of his efforts concentrated on how he could see Mel again, how he could make her understand that he was back for good and that whatever had happened in the last few months could be put away and forgotten about. He couldn't imagine a future without her or indeed any type of future at all.

43

He stumbled upon his sister in Tanners Park. She was with a bunch of other lasses. They were sat on the swings in the dark, wrapped up against the snow in hoodies and scarves. The park was covered in a clean and fresh layer but the snow around the swings was trampled and ugly beneath their feet. They were passing cigarettes around, smoke and steam coming from their mouths. They had two huge bottles of cider and they were doing the same with them, passing each around from one to the next, taking swigs. Every now and then, when the wind came at him, he heard their voices, shrill and brittle in the cold. He heard the language they were using and the things they were talking about and he saw that his sister was the most obvious there, the one who was drinking the most, the one who had the most to say. Sometimes he could make out her voice from the others. He heard the word 'army' and realised she was talking about him so he crept closer. They didn't see him, had no idea that he was there listening to it all.

His sister carried on shouting.

'He's ruined everything. Mam's lost it. Terry hardly comes by any more. You've seen her. She doesn't even know what day it is. Why did he do it? He's a selfish bastard. He shouldn't have gone. Just out of school. He was too young to go. You heard what Saunders said. You spend five years of your life trying to make something of somebody and then this happens. He started to cry in front of me. Can you imagine Saunders crying?'

She started crying herself then, her words breaking apart. Two of the girls went to her and hugged her, holding on tight, fighting her when she tried to break free. One of them started crying, too. One of the cider bottles was on the ground by his sister's feet. He saw her kick it over in anger. The cider sprayed out of the bottle and the bottle span in circles on the icy slush before coming to a stop on its side. The rest of the cider came glugging out of the bottle in pulses, each pulse weakening until there was no pulse left.

All he could do was watch. He didn't have the nerve to approach them. He didn't understand what was happening but he knew the worst thing he could possibly do was to go over to his sister now in this place and try to make amends for whatever it was he'd done. But what had he done that was so wrong? Joined the army? Left home for six months? Been sent to a foreign land? Fought in a war? Done his duty? None of those things were crimes. If anybody should be feeling ashamed it was his family, for leaving him to fester in a hospital bed, for not coming to see him, for not understanding that he'd left to better himself. But seeing his sister made his mind up about going home. He was frightened to go there, of seeing his mam, of not being welcomed the way he'd dreamed it.

Scottie came to be in a room full of people. Out of the ceiling came a purple light that flashed in many colours, flickered golden and then white. It descended to the place where Scottie was and then it stopped above him. He felt a mass of sensations, incredible things happening to his nerve endings until his whole body was tingling. Out of the light came the face of Jesus. It terrified him and he backed away from it.

A moment later and Scottie was in an underground car park. It was filled to waist height with rotting flesh and blood. Dogs were swimming in it. He could hear the looter screaming, the man's voice echoing and reverberating in the darkness. He searched desperately for a way out, located a white door and made his way to it. When he opened the door he was back in the real world again, staring into the eyes of the girl, the classroom freezing cold, the pain in his shoulder agonising, all-consuming.

44

It was past midnight when he reached The Thistle. He was cold and needed somewhere warm to go that wasn't home. Lights were on upstairs where Dougie lived but the downstairs lights were off and the front door locked. He snuck over the back fence and clicked open the door to the hallway, knowing it wouldn't be locked, knowing Dougie's habits too well. The door to the bar was open too. Scottie pushed through it and stopped still in the shadows. Dougie's Alsatian was there. The dog moved in its basket, breathed heavily, sniffed at the air and then slumped down again.

Scottie stepped forward. As soon as he did the dog started barking, softly at first then madly, working itself up, whirling in circles. It had never been scared of him before. The lads had always joked about it. They were terrified of the thing and it knew it. It frightened the life out of them every time they came across it, but it had never been like that with Scottie. It had always gone up to him and rolled on to its back, stuck its legs in the air.

'Soft as shite,' Dougie used to say but Dougie had loved him for it and even tried to get him taking the thing for walks. The dog always looked like it might bite someone else though and Scottie didn't want a part of that so he'd turned Dougie down. Now the dog was scared of him. It was clear to see. It's heckles were up and whatever fear it felt had consumed it. It backed off to the corner of the room, continuing its barking, showing its teeth. Scottie stood stock still, staring at the wall above the fireplace. The photograph there showed him smiling on the day of his passing-out parade. He was in his dress uniform, standing tall and proud, back straight, chest pushed forward, looking the part. It meant something. It meant all the things his mam and sister understood and it meant all the other things that they could never understand. There were other photos too, his uncle in the wheelchair, Scottie kneeling beside him, a big, broad smile on his uncle's face, his hand on Scottie's shoulder, gripping it. His mam smiling. All the lads together, bundling into the shot. The day had been a scream.

A door slammed and the sound of footsteps moved down the stairs. Scottie ducked into the corner beneath the dartboard just as Dougie appeared in the bar. Dougie switched on the light and stared across the room, shouting. He looked a mess, like he'd just woken. For the briefest second Scottie thought Dougie had seen him, but then Dougie started across the room away from him towards the dog, calmed it down, fussed over it until it settled. Scottie watched him, unable to step out of the shadows, too scared of what might happen if he did. It didn't matter that this was Dougie, one of his uncle's oldest friends. It didn't matter that he'd spent more hours in The Thistle in the last three years than any other pub in the city. He simply couldn't bring himself to speak. Instead he slipped away to the door and out of the place, his head a mess.

He clambered over the back wall, feet slipping and made off through the estate to his uncle's place. He found the key where his mam always left it, let himself in. Afraid to turn the light on, afraid of being discovered, he dropped on to the old sofa in the living room, the pain in his shoulder coming in waves, his breathing shallow and laboured. He started having ideas, no one thing forming into a whole but everything leading in the same direction. He had to do something, something that would cause a stir, something that would get a reaction. He lay still in the darkness, just the orange glow of the streetlights for company, staring at the window and the gentle snowfall; lay encased in loneliness until sleep converged on him.

The classroom quiet, the warm comfort of orange street lamps at the windows, the two of them in the darkness. She wouldn't stop staring at him and wouldn't let him rest.

'What do you think happens?' she asked.

'When?'

'When people die.'

'I don't care,' he said. 'I've seen death. I don't want to think about it.'

'I've seen death too,' she said. 'And I know what happens after-wards.'

'How do you know?'

He turned to the window. Sunlight was seeping over the hills.

'It already happened,' she said.

'What are you talking about?' he shouted.

'We're the same,' she said.

'We are not the same.'

'You'll see,' she said. 'Soon enough.'

He tried to ignore her, but she was having none of it.

'Okay then,' she said. 'It's like floating, or swimming under water.'

He turned towards her, trying to work out what game she was playing.

'It was just a normal day,' she said. 'I always caught the bus.'

'What are you talking about?' he said. He knelt up at the win-dow. There was still nobody. It didn't make sense.

'The sun was shining. There were joggers in the park. I was on the bus like always. There was the loudest noise. Everything went black. Immediately I was floating . . . or swimming . . . you know,

like everything was lighter. And then a kind of hollow sound filled my head, like being underwater. The people around me started to drift off in different directions, leaving their screams behind, but I didn't move. I couldn't. The blackness lifted at that exact moment and I could see the truth of it all, how the bus had opened up like a tin can, how there were bits of the bus all over the road and in the park and somewhere I could hear more screaming and shouting but it was very distant, hardly real . . .'

'Stop!' he shouted. 'I don't want to listen to you. I don't want you to speak.'

'You know I'm right,' she said. 'You know it's true.'

He shook his head.

'This is real,' he said. 'I can feel you. I can see you. What are you?'

'I saw you at the train station,' she said. 'I saw what you were, that you were the same as me, so I followed you.'

'I don't get it,' he said.

'I didn't get it either,' she said. 'When it happened I thought I was the same as everybody else, wandering around the place in a daze. But everybody from the rear of the bus where I was sitting had gone except for me. I was left behind.'

He ran back to the window. He didn't hide. He didn't care any more who might be out there or what they might do to him if he showed himself.

But there was nobody out there. The car park was empty.

'Nobody's coming,' she said. 'It's just you and me.

'It's weird,' he said. 'I can't actually remember how I got here.'

'It doesn't matter,' she said. 'Because it's not really happening.'

In that instant, out of nowhere, a blinding white light filled the room. He had to cover his eyes. When he tried to move back from the window he stumbled and fell. He didn't feel the same, the room full of light, the girl somewhere and nowhere. He could hear shouting, angry voices, the humming of engines, the same madness as in the town, distant gunfire, smashing glass, explosions that were close, too close, and yet not so close, not really, the whiteness softening everything. He tried to get up but had no feeling in his legs and when he did finally rise it was not the same. He was floating, or swimming. It felt more like swimming. He saw something lying on the ground. It was covered in dust, surrounded by debris, shards of glass and spent shell casings. He had to look away from it, was disgusted by it. A crumpled body. A uniform he recognised, one of the lads who'd been sitting next to him in the truck just a moment before. He collapsed to the floor in the classroom, sensed the girl leaning over him. He crawled to the window. A police helicopter was hovering outside, its spotlight trained on the alleyways outside the school. For a moment Scottie thought they'd discovered him but as quickly as it appeared the helicopter moved off again, its searchlights seeking some other lost soul for some pathetic reason.

45

It was snowing faster when he next looked out of the window, heavy flakes falling from a white, shapeless sky. He thought he could hear a rumbling sound like tanks on a tarmac road, moving ever closer, a sound that threatened to carry him from one place to another so that he had to pinch himself to stop it happening again. There was always the fear that somehow he might be transported back there. It caught him cold and gripped him tightly until he found even the basic act of breathing difficult, and as he fought to catch a breath so the grip tightened, as a snake tightens around its prey and crushes the very life out of it, as body armour compresses a chest that is struggling to work as nature intended.

He was curled up inside his uncle's old place, watching the snow fall from the window. The downstairs furniture was as it had always been, the same musty smell, the same ornaments on the mantelpiece, the same discoloured netting in the windows. His mam had been busy here but nothing much had changed. He got up from the sofa and pulled the netting back. His uncle's house was opposite the school. It was mid-morning and he could see the kids in their lessons. A teacher came to one of the top windows and stared out of it. The room was high and on the corner of the building. It was where he wanted to be later, after he'd done what he had to do. They'd know he'd selected it so he had an arc of fire. They'd be forced to take him seriously.

Scottie left the window and went upstairs. Most of the stuff was in boxes. His mam was taking a long time with it all, packing things precisely, labelling and organising. Two of the rooms were empty. The third room, the one that had been his uncle's bedroom, only half-finished. The bed was gone and the chest of drawers but the old oak wardrobe was still by the window. Scottie went over to it. There were boxes stacked in there and old photo albums. The rifle was still inside too, propped up in a corner.

After he'd checked the rifle he sat himself on the floor in the shadows and waited for the day to end and night to begin, all of his thoughts trained on Mel and the bloke she was seeing. It was Friday, going-out night. In the space of an hour, cradling the rifle through it all, he relived his entire relationship with Mel. Individual moments fell into his head as the snowflakes fell beyond the window; Mel waiting for him at the school gates when they first started going out; their first kiss; the first time they'd gone beyond kissing; eating Chinese food on Friday nights like this one, bringing a takeaway home for her mam, the two of them sitting up watching crap TV together, laughing, her heading off to bed, him crashing out on the sofa until the sun was streaming through the windows, then trying to get up so Mel could go to the hairdresser's on a Saturday or, if it was a Sunday, her mam to church.

It should have been happening just like that today. It was a part of both of them. It was the way of things. Instead he was stuck in his uncle's old house. The heating had been turned off, the water too. He was freezing cold and desperate for a drink. He stroked the butt of the rifle for comfort, all the while fighting back tears and feelings of nausea. Every now and again his shoulder flared up. There was nothing he could do but grit his teeth and wait for it to pass. He picked up one of the photo albums and opened it. There were pictures inside from when his uncle was in the army, keepsakes from the Falklands, postcards and badges and other stuff. There was an envelope too. On the front his uncle had written a note to himself. It said 'found on body of Argentine soldier'. Inside were a series of pictures, young men laughing and smiling at the camera, showing off, holding their weapons in the air. Later the pictures changed. There were shots of explosions and wrecked equipment. The last photo showed one of the lads that had been in the early photos. He was lying on his back, neck twisted at an impossible angle, mouth open, dark eyes staring blankly at nothing. Scottie looked at it for a long time, turning it over in his fingers, then he put it in his pocket and put the rest of the photos and the album back in the wardrobe.

By the time the hour ticked by he was a wreck, his head full of questions he needed answering and processes he couldn't cope with. The biggest one was about Mel and this new lad. Somewhere deep inside him was the fluttering fear that she'd take the lad back home for Chinese takeaway. Somewhere inside was the fear that her mam would be laughing and that he could be replaced so easily, that years meant nothing, that the past was history already and of no concern.

He picked himself off the floor and made his way to the front door. There was only one way of knowing and that was to find her. If he found her with him, if they looked like they were heading back to her place then he'd have to deal with it. He had the rifle after all.

He watched her sleeping, the light of dawn coming in strips through the window, dust hanging in the air in the light. He watched her breathing. She was real. Everything was real, but there was something missing, some emphatic thing missing from inside of him, missing from the room, missing from the world.

Frustrated, he kicked her awake.

'Okay, then,' he said. 'What about those birds on the wire out there. Are they real? Of course they are. What about the sunrise? What about the horizon?'

'It's real,' she said. 'But you're not in it, not part of it.'

'What about Mel? How do you explain that?'

'It never happened.'

'Of course it happened. I spoke to her. That's what started this whole thing off.'

'That happened in your head. You invented it.'

'So she's not seeing that lad? She hasn't dumped me? The other night never happened? I didn't hit him? Is that what you're saying?'

'I don't know what she's doing or what's happening between you two,' she said. 'I can't tell you those things.'

He laughed.

'You don't know anything. I know more than you do.'

A silence.

'I know soon enough you're going to understand, Scottie,' she said. 'I know it's hard but it'll become clear in the end.'

He turned toward her.

'See? Even that doesn't make any sense. How do you know my name? This is madness. I was injured. They sent me home. Everything was fine until I got off the train but now . . .   '

'But you felt it,' she said. 'In the hospital, you felt it there.'

'Felt what?'

'The emptiness. The loneliness. The coldness. All those things.'

'I got confused, that's all. It makes sense. I was tired. I'm still recovering.'

'Recovering from what?' she asked.

'My injuries, of course.'

'What injuries?'

'These injuries. Do you want to see? Is that what you want?'

He tore his jacket off and started at his shirt buttons, turned to show her his back.

'Don't,' she said.

'Why not? Afraid I'll prove you wrong, show you how I know you're a fake?'

But what he saw took his breath away because there was no injury to his shoulder. There were no scars either, just his clean, white skin.

He shook his head.

'I can still feel the pain from it,' he said. 'I'm not imagining it. It's real.'

'You're remembering it,' she said. 'If you stop fighting it the pain will go away.'

'I don't believe any of this,' he said. 'I don't believe this is happening.'

'That's because it isn't,' she said. 'If you give up whatever it is you're trying to do it will all just go away. You can rest and I can rest too.'

'I don't want to rest,' he said. 'I've got things to do here. I . . .'

He stopped talking. He'd run out of words to say about it.

'Just leave me,' he said.

He turned to the window.

'I can't,' she said. 'I'm stuck with you until this is over.'

He dropped to his haunches against the wall, too tired to argue anymore.

'Suit yourself,' he said. 'Just don't talk to me. I'm finished with talking.'

46

After dark, not knowing where else to go, Scottie left the school and headed home. The girl followed him. He was too tired to try to stop her. She trudged along behind him in the snow, shivering. He let her shiver. He didn't want her there.

His mother was in the kitchen when he arrived at his house. She was at the sink, staring down the garden to the shed. He stopped short on the garden path. She was there in front of him but she did not see him or react and he knew that it was true. She could not see him because nobody could see him. He was beginning to understand this.

'Find direction for what's missing,' whispered the girl.

'What?'

'All that energy needs a place to spend itself.'

'What energy?'

'Love?'

He turned to look at her, wondering what planet she was from.

'What's she doing?' he asked.

'Waiting.'

'Waiting for what?'

'Waiting for you.'

He shook his head.

'I'm lost,' he said. 'I don't think I can handle much more of this.'

'No, you're not. You're home,' said the girl.

'So what now? What good is any of this if I can't speak to anybody? What good is it if they can't see me?

'I think you missed where you were meant to go to,' she said. 'I've been through all of this already. All the things you're doing. All the things you're feeling. I've done them all and felt them all. My parents aren't together any more. After what happened to me they just gave up. I watched it happen.'

'How long?' Scottie asked.

'How long what?'

'How long did it take, for them to break up?'

'A year.'

'You've been waiting and watching for a year?'

'Longer now,' she said. 'Too long.'

'Then why don't you go to wherever *you're* supposed to be?' asked Scottie.

'I was going,' she said. 'I'd made my mind up to leave. I felt just like you feel now. Then I saw you on the train. I don't even know why I was on that train. You made me think about how I was when it first happened, how lost I felt and something just told me to follow you, to see . . .'

'To see what?'

'If you needed help. It's a good job I did.'

'I don't see how you work that one out,' said Scottie. 'I don't see what help you've been to me.'

'If you'd not had me around you wouldn't know what you were doing. Think about those first few hours.'

'I was doing okay,' he said.

'Wandering around outside the cemetery? Stalking your ex-girlfriend? Breaking in to places?'

'I had to know some things.'

'You were filling the gaps,' she said. 'But you had no idea. You didn't know what was real and what was in your head. What about the school? What were you doing there? If I hadn't come along you'd still be in there sulking because your big plan failed. You'd still be thinking you'd hit that lad and the whole world was out to get you.'

'It wasn't a plan, not really. It wasn't anything at all. It just happened. I didn't know what I was doing.'

'There, you said it,' she said.

He stopped talking. It was pointless arguing.

His mam left the kitchen, turning out the light as she went. Darkness flooded the back lawn and trapped them in its folds. He stood for a moment, looking at her, her skin smooth in the moonlight, her face so perfectly shaped.

'Follow me,' he said.

The girl looked at him, questioning.

'I need you to stay with me,' he said. 'I need your help.'

'On one condition,' she said.

'What's that?'

'That when it's all over, we go to the garden together.'

He thought about the garden and the man at the hospital. It scared him. But what choice did he have? He couldn't go on like this forever. Not forever.

Scottie turned to the shed, walked up the path toward it, opened the door. Inside everything was as it always had been. He stood in the doorway thinking about the last time he'd been here, the night he'd spent with Mel, the thunderstorm. He looked up at the ceiling, at the nails he'd hammered. Tears welled in his eyes and it took all of his remaining energy to stop himself from crying in front of the girl and making things worse.

'We'll stay here tonight,' he said. 'You can have one of the beds but I'm sleeping there.'

'I don't need to sleep,' she said. 'You don't need to sleep.'

He walked to the sofa and dropped down on it.

'I need to be here,' he said. 'Please?'

The girl made her way across the shed to the bunks and sat down.

'Thanks,' he said.

He lay back on the sofa, breathing in its smell, curled himself up into the back of it and closed his eyes on the world, not caring about the specifics, just enjoying the feel of it, real or imagined.

47

Drew's house was in the middle of the row. Scottie hopped over the back fence just like he had a million times before. The girl followed him. It was not long after dawn. Snow was still sitting in patches on the lawn, a sheet hanging on the washing line and a pair of work trousers, a pair of black boots leaning against the back doorstep.

The house was still. Scottie stepped back and looked upward. The curtains were closed in Drew's room.

'Wait here,' he said.

The girl shrugged her shoulders, went over to a low wall and sat down on it, not caring about the snow. Scottie watched her for a moment, wondering, then he turned to the house again.

The back door was unlocked. The musty smell of Drew's dogs hit him when he entered the kitchen, but the dogs didn't come hammering through the house to greet him like they usually did and the smell was more than just dogs. There was a staleness in the air, a coldness, and he sensed it immediately. Scottie moved through the kitchen into the hall. There was a coldness here too. Drew's house had always been a mad place, a place full of life. It had never been like this, never so empty of being, the front room empty of atmosphere, the little red standby lights of the DVD and TV staring at him from the corner like two tired eyes, a half-drunk mug of cold tea on the table, cigarette butts in the ashtray.

Scottie moved along the hall and started to climb the stairs, feeling the banister in his palms, thinking about tearing up and down the same stairs as a kid, running with Drew from his big sister, Leslie, trying to get her wound up so she chased them. He remembered having a crush on her when they were at primary school and how jealous he was when she went to the big school and got a boyfriend there. He even remembered the boyfriend's name. Brian. Years later he took the piss out of her about it.

'Brian, Brian, oh Brian.'

She laughed. She had two kids and was shacked up with the father of the latest over in Govan. She made jokes about him joining the army and told him if he turned up on her doorstep in his uniform there was a chance she might not be able to resist him. He joked that he'd be there and sometimes he'd secretly wondered what might happen if he actually did turn up one time when her bloke was at work, stand there in the doorway in his finest.

The landing was quiet, Drew's door half-open. Scottie moved silently towards it. Drew's room was the same as it had always been. He could make out the shape of Drew on the bed. He was laid out flat on his back in his Hoops shirt, his eyes closed, breathing steadily. Scottie crept across the carpet to his bedside, leaned in close. He wanted to reach out and give him a shove, give him a scare, wake him and share a joke, but something held him back. Would Drew know him?

Scottie crept over to the window, pulled back the curtains an inch. He looked down into the yard. The girl was still there, sat on the wall. She was stroking a cat. It could be done then.

A book was lying on the table by Drew's bed, sat on top of a Hoops programme. Scottie laughed at the thought of Drew reading a book and picked it up to see. The cover showed a light emerging from darkness. At the bottom were three words written in gold.

'Why People Die.'

Scottie dropped the book. It fell to the table, teetered there a second and then fell again to the floor. Drew started to wake. Scottie raced from the room and on to the landing, down the stairs through the kitchen to the yard. He heard Drew shouting.

'Mam! Mam! Is that you?'

When the girl saw Scottie she jumped to her feet.

'Well?' she asked.

'We need to leave right now,' he said. 'I made a mistake.'

48

Mist hanging like a grey veil in the bare branches of the trees, the trees dark and spectral in the afternoon light, Scottie and the girl in the cemetery. The snow had piled itself on to every surface, softened the edges of the stones, making the picture before him confusing. It was difficult to see where the walkways ran between the graves, difficult to see where the borders began. People had visited, but the new covering of snow had extinguished almost all trace of them. The flowers at his uncle's grave were covered in snow and had wilted under the weight. Tiny traces of colour broke through the white blanket; red and yellow; purple and pink.

He stood for a time at the grave, thinking, snatching at moments and reliving them, remembering the time when his uncle had lived away from the city, the trips he'd made to the country to see him, the things they'd done together, the happy days before the drink and memories got a hold; digging in the allotment; shelling peas; walking in the woods; spying deer in the shadows; picking blackberries; conkers; heading down to the quarry; fossil hunting; to the park; cricket matches on summer Sundays; fishing at the pond; summer fetes; until the moments were snatched back just as the city had snatched his uncle back, dragged him back into its very guts and finished him off.

Pressing his hands deep into his pockets, Scottie moved away to the pond. It was frozen over, the ice covered in snow.

He thought about walking out on to it, thought about the ice creaking, groaning, cracking under his weight, thought about falling through it, to water. In his head was the image of the soldier in the garden, wires dangling from his arms, the soldier raising his head to look through the window, the face becoming his uncle's face, the snow melting around him, the garden blossoming to flower.

The girl was sat on a bench by the cemetery wall, slumped forwards. She looked up as he approached and then dropped her gaze when she saw that he'd seen her. He ignored her at first, got as far as the gate, had the cold metal in his grip before stopping.

'I'm going,' he said. 'There's nothing here.'

'Where to now?' she asked.

'I don't know,' he said. 'Some place. Somewhere else. Anywhere.'

She looked up at him.

'Can I come with you?'

He nodded.

'If you want. Are you cold?'

'Yes,' she said.

'It's not the weather, is it?'

'No,' she said.

'But I can feel it.'

'Yes, but it's not the weather.'

The gate squeaked as he pulled it open.

'I'm going to my uncle's house,' he said. 'It's the only place I feel real. I'm going to think things through. You can come if you want.'

'You believe me though. After today, you believe me?'

'I don't know what to believe,' he said. 'I believe you but I don't. I could be dreaming. I could be in a coma, something like that. I could be imagining the whole thing. Have you been crying?'

She grimaced.

'It's nothing,' she said. 'Part of me wants to go back to the garden, like if I go there now all of this will be over, and part of me wants to stay with you.'

'Why?' he asked. 'Why would you want to stay with me?'

'I don't know,' she said. 'I can't explain it. It's like a job I have to finish.'

'Well, don't hold your breath,' he said.

He led her out of the cemetery and up Hillside, walking in slush against the traffic so that each step felt laboured and heavy. When they reached the crossroads he stopped and stared at the hairdresser's across the way. The lights were off. The dark glass threw the bright reflections of car headlights back at him. He stood for a moment more, thinking about Mel, trying to contain himself, then he turned and made his way towards his uncle's house, the girl trudging behind him, turning sharply every now and then as the cars sped past them, sometimes startled, sometimes only remembering, reliving a moment of her own.

The lights were on when they arrived. He stood at the window, looking in. The girl stepped up beside him. After a while his mother appeared. She was clearing boxes.

'We can't stay here,' he said. 'Not yet.'

They walked back to Hillside and continued upward until the shops petered out, the houses and street lights too.

'Where are we going?' she asked.

'Anywhere,' he said.

'Come with me,' she said. 'Please.'

He was crossing the road when she said it and he stopped now, right in the middle.

'I don't want to go with you. I don't want to go anywhere. I want to stay here. Right here.'

He repeated the words over and over to himself.

'This whole thing's a joke,' he shouted. 'It's a joke!'

His voice disappeared into the dark folds of black beyond

the city, was muffled by soft snow until it was as though he had no voice at all.

No cars were coming. He sat down on the tarmac, leant back until he was flat against it, staring up at the stars. He felt the gritty wetness on the side of his face.

'How can I feel it? If I'm not here how can I feel it?'

A car came up the hill, headlights growing bigger by the second, the rush and hiss of its tyres on the wet road growing louder and louder. A vision of the looter appeared, confusion and bewilderment written on his face. The looter started laughing hysterically.

Scottie started laughing too.

'Bring it on,' he shouted. 'Bring it on!'

The girl watched him.

'What if I don't move?' he asked her. 'What if I stay right here?'

She shrugged her shoulders.

Scottie waited a moment more until the car was almost on top of him and then he rolled to the pavement. The car rushed past his head, missing it by inches. He lay there on the roadside, panting for breath, holding back tears, the weight of everything slamming down on him. The girl crossed the road and sat down on the kerb beside him. She put a hand on his face. Ahead of him, the road disappeared into the darkness. He watched the red lights of the car blinking back at him until they disappeared too. He didn't know what he was doing or where he was going. There was nothing ahead, no answers, just the pitch black road. He could walk it forever and it wouldn't get him anywhere.

'Please come to the garden,' she said.

'Why?' he asked.

'Because it's better than here,' she said. 'It's better than this.'

'What if I say no?' he asked.

'I don't know,' she said. 'You keep walking and it goes on and on . . .'

'I want to settle everything first,' he said. 'Then I'll come to your garden.'

'There's nothing to settle,' she said.

'There is,' he said. 'There's everything.'

She shook her head.

'No,' she said. 'Not any more.'

He thought about the place he'd been, the dust, the looter in the street, Mel. Anger welled up inside of him.

'I need to see Mel,' he said. 'I need to sort out what she's playing at.'

'In the way you already imagined?' asked the girl. 'By beating someone up?'

'Not just anyone,' he said. 'The lad that stole her from me.'

'A person can't steal another person like that,' she said. Then she stopped talking for a while. In the end she said, 'I don't believe that anyway.'

He shook his head for an unnaturally long time, the anger boiling, threatening to blow.

'If I can open doors and climb stairs and touch things that are real I can sort him out.'

'You don't want to do that,' she said. 'That's just mad talk.'

'Yes, I do,' he said. 'You don't know me. You don't know how it makes me feel to think about them together.'

'And then what happens afterwards?' she asked him. 'What happens after you've hit him or whatever it is you're planning?'

'Then she'll know,' he said. 'Then she'll see.'

He stood upright before her, pushing his chest forward, not feeling his shoulder, the rage inside him forcing its way out.

'And then?'

He stood still for a moment, his head full of thoughts.

'I don't care,' he said. He turned and ran from her, using the strategy he'd always used, not remotely aware of it, ran away from the darkness, back to where the street lights and houses began, back to the place he'd called home for seventeen years. He didn't stop running until he was at Mel's house. He saw that the lights were off and nobody was there so he ran on, down into the middle of town. What snow was left had turned to slush, dirty salt piled against the kerbs, the pavements wet but no longer slippery, the orange street lights shining on the concrete, the lights of the bars and pubs reflecting there too.

She was in one of the swanky new wine bars, sat with a lad with blond hair. The place was quiet, the two of them on their own, drinks on the table in front of them. She had her hair done up and make-up on and even though he was outside of the window Scottie felt he could smell her, not just her perfume but the very scent of her being. There were two bouncers on the door. They hadn't seen him so he knew nothing had changed. He stood with his face pressed to the wet glass. He wanted to crash right though it there and then, end their little party, see Mel's face when she realised what was happening. He clenched his fists and thought about putting one through the window, thought about butting the window with his forehead, kicking the window, doing anything to break his way through. In the end he settled on half a brick that was sitting in the slush against the kerb. He held it in the palm of his right hand, letting the ice melt to water and drip through his fingers. He knocked the brick against his thigh, moved from one foot to the other in agitation, building up to throw it. The bouncers were none the wiser. A middle-aged couple walked right past him. They had no idea he was there. He was about to throw the brick when Mel and the lad got up out of their seats. Scottie watched through the glass as they

walked towards the doorway. And then the bottom fell out of
Scottie's world.

The lad with Mel was Drew.

His legs faltering, Scottie dropped back into the shadows.
He didn't understand what he was seeing. Mel and Drew.
They left the bar and turned to walk towards him. Mel and
Drew. Drew and Mel. His girl and his best friend. His best
friend and his girl. He had one thing on his mind now, to wait
until they passed him, then he was going to take the brick and
smash it into Drew's skull, smash it hard until the bone
cracked, payback for all the years of love and friendship he was
seeing ripped apart in front of his eyes. He could hardly contain himself. He was going to make everything real, make his
statement once and for all. He was hot-wired, ready-set,
almost overcome with the thought of what he was going to
do, but when they stepped into the pool of light from the bar
Scottie noticed things beyond the black rage in his head. They
weren't touching each other. They weren't smiling. Mel had
her arms folded against the cold. She was walking with her
head down. She seemed to be only half-there. Drew was the
same, not saying anything, not laughing or joking, not doing
anything, just walking next to her, his hands buried deep in his
pockets. Scottie saw that Mel had been crying. Her eyes were
red and puffy. He saw Drew looking at her, saw him step sideways towards her, adjusting his stride to match hers, saw him
lift an arm to her shoulder. Mel leant into it and Drew pulled
her towards him. There was nothing Scottie could do but
watch the two of them. The realisation that this was two
people comforting each other, that this was what Mel needed
and what Drew needed, hit him in the chest even as he lifted
the brick to strike. There was nothing he could do after that
because the anger he had been feeling collapsed into a heap
inside of him. A new feeling rose up to take its place, a feeling
of absolute love for them both, a desperate need to see them

happy, to see her cared for even if it was without him, even if it was with someone else. He knew then that it was over.

He dropped the brick to the ground and waited in the shadows to let them pass, then he watched them make their way towards the taxis that were parked at the end of the block, feeling things come to an end but knowing the end had already happened weeks before when the news had come that the boy Mel had first connected with on a trampoline when she was fourteen years old, the boy Drew had first met on a rainy September break-time at primary school, had been killed by a roadside bomb in a country that was foreign to each of them in every conceivable way.

Scottie watched Mel climb into the taxi, watched Drew make sure she got in safely. Then Drew crossed the road and walked away, leaving Scottie in the shadows, an invisible being without form, a ghost from another time. Without thinking Scottie ran to the taxi, jumping in before Mel closed the door, needing the moment, needing the closeness. He sat next to her as the taxi made its way out of the city centre and back to the estate, just watching her, transmitting every ounce of love he felt for her into her being, hoping that somehow she would feel it and understand. Her hand was resting on the seat. He reached out to touch her, moved his fingers within an inch of hers and then stopped, too scared to go through with it, too confused as to what might happen. He looked at her face, saw how red her eyes were from crying. There was nothing he could do to stop her feeling that way. When the taxi pulled up outside her house he climbed out after her and then he let her go away from him, stood at the gate and watched her close her front door, felt the silence all around him after she'd gone. He knew in that instant that he was in the wrong place, was clinging to something that was gone forever, something that could never be replaced.

49

The girl was already at the shed when he arrived. He dropped on to the sofa beside her and told her all that had happened.

'Now will you come?' she asked.

'I have to see my mam,' he said. 'Properly. Not just watch her. Then I'll come.'

They walked up the garden path together and in through the kitchen door, stood there watching his mam as she fussed. The kitchen was a mess, dishes piled high in the sink, the bin full of rubbish, tea stains on the work surfaces, the sort of kitchen his mam would never keep. He couldn't understand it, why she was keeping his uncle's place so immaculate but letting this place go to the dogs. After making tea she went upstairs and into Scottie's room. Scottie and the girl went into the living room. It was the same story in there, the place in a state, used plates and glasses on the coffee table, letters and newspapers strewn across the floor. Scottie fought hard to keep it together. He hadn't expected this. It was like his mam had stopped living in the place, like she'd given up on all the things that kept her busy. He climbed the stairs quickly, more worried for her now than he had been.

She was in his room, sat on the edge of the bed. The room was spotless, the bed made, the carpet clean, Scottie's things laid out. His mam picked up a photograph and started talking to it. The words came softly and she spoke to the photograph as if she were speaking directly to her lost son.

'I felt it at your passing-out parade. Everybody was cheering and clapping but that wasn't the whole story. There was something else there with us, hidden behind all the smiles and laughter. At first I could only see it in the other women but then I saw it in the men too. I thought to myself 'it's just a little thing' but after a while I realised it wasn't a little thing at all. It was a big thing we'd all caught hold of. It was going to slow us down. There you all were, beaming faces, all set for your big adventure and we were happy for you, but all the parents were thinking the same, "Why did I agree to this? What sort of a parent am I? What if the worst happens?"'

She turned the photograph over in her hands and Scottie saw it was one from his parade, the same photo as the one in The Thistle. There he was, uniform pristine, huge smile, laughing and grappling with the others, the sun shining.

'I was dead proud,' whispered his mam. 'I was made up to see you in your uniform, my son, my little boy becoming a man, and I could see what it meant to you and how proud you were of yourself. The army was doing you good, I could see that. You never really had a dad. I know there's Terry and I know he tries but Terry's never really been a dad to you . . . a dad to your sister maybe but not to you. You were just that little bit too old when he came along. I always felt you suffer for that, that it shrunk you down despite your size. I wondered if you were forever making up for that with your jokes and laughter. But the army made you just that little bit taller still. I could see it. It was something only a mam could ever see; still it was hard to look at you, son. I was filled with love and pride but also fear and it was the same for all the other parents. I'm certain of that. You make a pact with yourself when your child joins the army. You tell yourself you're never going to think the worst and you tell yourself you're never going to worry. You're never going to think about the future either because you don't want to tempt fate so you try not to look forward to your son coming home, just in case. And when you write your letters you take care not to mention how worried you are. I used to read those letters back to myself a hundred times and I'd end up writing ten before I got one that was okay to send. I filled them with news about what your sister was up to or what was happening in the neighbourhood, silly things really that you probably weren't the least bit interested in. But you were my only son, my first born, and now look at you . . .'

She was crying now. It was more than he could stand.

'I can't sleep, Scottie,' she said. 'I just see a picture of you lying in that road. I imagine you waiting for me to come to you. I imagine you as a baby and as a little boy. I imagine you calling for me.'

'Mam! Mam!'

He was shouting at the top of his lungs but his voice faltered and broke under the strain.

'She can't hear you,' said the girl.

Scottie raised his hand and held it in front of her.

'Or see you. She doesn't know you're here.'

'Then I need to show her,' he said.

She grabbed him.

'No! Please! You shouldn't!'

'Then why are we here? What's the point if she doesn't know.'

'Maybe she wants you to listen,' said the girl.

'But I can't let her know I'm okay. I can't tell her like I couldn't tell Mel and Drew. There's no point in any of this.'

The girl stared at Scottie, tears forming in the wells of her eyes.

'Try,' said the girl. 'Think of something else.'

For the longest time Scottie stood there, his mam sitting on the bed in front of him, staring at the picture, running her fingers across it. He couldn't bear to watch her, couldn't leave her this way. He summoned all of his remaining strength in an effort to break through to her, not caring what the girl had to say about it. And then understanding broke over him in a powerful wave as he thought of the blueys. He felt in his pocket, found the letters tucked away there, creased and dog-eared but the words inside them hadn't changed.

'These are all I have,' he said.

The girl nodded and smiled at him.

'It's the best way,' she said. 'I promise.'

His mam went through to her own room, closed the curtains and climbed under the covers. Scottie followed her to the doorway and then watched her as she tried to get some sleep. The room was dark. There was the hum of the central heating, the clanging in the pipes, the atmosphere heavy and heady, the way she liked it to be. When he was sure she was drifting away he crept up to her. He placed his hand on her forehead. He couldn't feel her and he knew she couldn't feel him so he tried to recall what it might feel like instead and willed for peace to find her anyway. He watched her breathing settle into a rhythm, her face lose the tension in it and begin to relax. He kissed her on the forehead, feeling nothing, and then made his way back to his bedroom. The girl was waiting for him. He took the letters from the pocket again.

'How?' he said.

'Just put them down,' she said.

'But it won't work. She won't see them,' he said.

'Yes, she will,' she said.

Scottie looked at the brand-new suitcase, each item of his uniform folded perfectly inside it.

'She'll know,' he said. 'Wherever I put them, she'll know. They'll all know.'

The girl smiled.

'They'll wonder,' she said. 'But they won't know. They'll never know.'

He opened the side zip on the suitcase and slid the envelopes into it, leaving the zip open an inch and the white corners showing, then he slipped quietly out of the room.

When they left the house the sky was clearer than ever, the moon shining down, causing the snow on the rooftops to shimmer and glisten like crystal.

'Come on now,' she said.

'I need to do one last thing,' he said. 'Tomorrow. I need to see them all right.'

She tilted her head and sighed.

'Please. Then I'm finished,' he said. 'Finished for good.'

50

He was waiting for Mel when she walked out of the house the next morning. He stood on the other side of the road, kept his distance. He understood better now, knew what was possible and what was not. He watched her pull on the red coat, the same one she'd worn on the night by the river, and tread her way tentatively down the slush-piled pathway to the gate, her breath forming little trails that faded to nothing in an instant. Her mother appeared in the doorway and followed behind. Scottie watched as the two of them linked arms on the pavement beyond the gate, Mel leaning in towards her mother, walking in step with her, the church bells ringing in the distance. He thought about her kneeling at the altar, lighting a candle for him, thinking of him and part of the old Scottie that was left inside yearned to witness that moment, as if he could take something from it, as if it would prove something, as if it would prove anything. But a larger part of him knew it was pointless carrying on, pointless chasing the shadow of the person he once was. He thought about leaving the St Christopher behind too, as he had left the letters for his mam to discover, but this was different. It would leave too many unanswered questions. He didn't know how exactly, but somehow he knew this to be wrong. Twisting the necklace in his fingers he followed the two of them as far as the alley that led to his mam's place and then he let Mel go for the last time, watched her disappear around the corner and out of his world forever. It was how things had to be from now on, final and forever.

51

He didn't reach his mam's. He was only just starting down the alley when he saw her coming the other way. She was striding along, looking like she had a place to be. He wondered if she was heading to church herself but she took herself off through the estate instead, walking with her head down, determined, towards the bus stop on Hillside. She caught a bus with an unfamiliar number, one he hadn't seen before. Following only his instinct, not thinking of his promise to the girl, he climbed on behind her. The bus made its way out of the city and into open countryside, almost empty of passengers, just his mam at the front behind the driver and a young couple on the back seat who looked like they were heading home from the night before. In the next town his mam changed for another bus. Scottie did the same. He knew where they were heading now though, worked it out from the road signs and the people who had climbed aboard. He felt a chill run through him, all the way through him, right to the core of his being.

It was a bright winter morning. The sky was blue, the air clean and fresh, just the smallest remnants of snow clinging to the shaded places where the sun couldn't penetrate but as the bus climbed steadily into the hills the snow became more dominant, the landscape changing in colour, turning white and featureless, the sky changing too, grey cloud and fog smothering everything until there was nothing to see from the

windows at all. All the while, Scottie's mam sat alone behind
the driver, looking down at her lap. Only when the bus
dropped into the next valley did the situation reverse itself,
and when it did Scottie caught sight of things familiar to him.
His heart skipped a beat, then another and another. They
were at the Regimental Headquarters, at the place where he
had performed his passing-out parade. The place was busy
too, full of people in civilian clothes. There were flags up,
banners lining the parade ground, crowds of people waiting
behind makeshift barriers. The sun came out and threw its
light on their faces.

The bus pulled to a stop. His mam went and stood on her
own beside the other mothers, the fathers, wives and children.
He knew what this was all about. They were here to witness
the regiment coming home and she was here to do the same.
He wondered if his letter had provoked it, could hardly
believe that he had chosen such a night to give it to her. She
didn't speak to anybody, just kept herself to herself, remained
on the edge of things. Scottie kept well away. He was in a
state of shock, unable to grasp what he was about to witness,
his mind in turmoil, his stomach doing cartwheels. He
couldn't stop himself from wondering all sorts of things. Who
was going to come home? Who wasn't? And all the while he
couldn't shake another thought from his being, that somewhere amidst all of this there might be another being like him,
another lost soul looking for something but not knowing what
that something was. He scoured the faces in the crowd, looking for the tell-tale signs but each and every face he focused on
looked like the one before it. None of them looked as he
knew he looked. None of them looked like the girl.

An hour passed before a cheer erupted from the crowd and
a line of coaches appeared at the gates. The coaches swung
around to a stop on the parade ground. Scottie could see lads
looking out of the windows, lads pointing and waving, lads on
their feet, reaching up to the racks above their heads, unable

to contain their eagerness to step into their old lives. There was a pause between the coaches pulling up and the doors opening and then the people waiting took small steps forward while slowly, tentatively, some like small boys stepping out of a dream, the lads appeared one by one into the sunlight. They appeared in ones, twos, threes and whole groups, their families rushing to greet them. Scottie watched his mam as she looked on, from a distance now, the crowd leaving her where she was stood, separating from her, mingling and merging with each other until she was on her own. Claps and cheers, tears of joy and relief and laughter floated across the concrete. He could only watch and do nothing, burning up inside for his mam, that she should have to go through this, but for all that there was the tiniest doubt about it all, because she had chosen to come here on this day, must have known about it, about how it would feel, what it would involve. It was this that kept him there. He had to know how it was going to turn out. He saw her take something from her bag. It was the letter he'd written, it had to be. He watched her open it, her fingers trembling and he watched her read it back to herself, right there on the tarmac. If he'd known of some way to breach the gulf between them he'd have done it then, at that precise moment, would have gladly given up eternity to make things better, but there was nothing he could do except look on, nothing, nothing at all except feel his heart bleeding for her.

And then something changed. It started with a movement in the crowd of people, a parting. From out of the confusion of faces one of the lads appeared. It was Atkinson. Behind him, one by one, came the others, McDonald, Robertson, the rest. They walked up to Scottie's mam and stopped in front of her and then in one sweeping movement, almost seamless, with no awkwardness at all, Atkinson stepped forward and hugged her. Scottie saw him whisper quietly into her ear. When she stepped away again she handed him the letter.

Atkinson read it as the lads stepped up to hug her in turn. Silently, unmoving, Scottie watched them. Atkinson reading his letter. The talks they'd had about it.

Somebody else appeared out of the crowd. Colton from Calton, struggling on his crutches. The lads welcomed him, some stepping forward to embrace him. Colton smiled and nodded back at them, almost there, almost part of it but Scottie saw something else too. It was like the faces of the squad players for the Hoops on a cup final day, there but not there as the other players paraded the trophy, part of things and not part of things. The lads moved back to Scottie's mam. Now Scottie could hear their words as they drifted gently across the parade ground to his ears. Words like 'solid' and 'the best'. He saw his mam smile and she carried that smile with her for the rest of the day, through all of the speeches and messages of condolence for the fallen, through the bus ride home and the final steps through the estate to her front door. He let her go then, just as he had let Mel go, made his way around the side of the house to the shed, the sky dark now, the temperature falling, understanding his time was almost at an end.

52

Drew and Mackie were in the shed when he got there. Highlights of a Hoops game were on the TV but the sound was down, neither of them really watching. They were supping lager from cans and chatting away about the things Mackie had been up to in the resort.

'You were right pissed at me,' said Mackie.

'It's because I didn't want you to stay,' said Drew. 'What else do you think it was about? I didn't want to go back to being stuck here every day on my own. I didn't want you to come back with your stories.'

'It was just a bar job. What did you think I was going to tell you about?'

'Anything. Everything. Being somewhere else. All I've had these past few months is the school. In the end I couldn't stand it.'

'You quit?'

'Yeah.'

'There are worse jobs, mate,' said Mackie. 'Believe me.'

'It wasn't the job,' said Drew. 'Not really. It was just weird being there. Especially since . . .'

Drew took another swig of lager.

'There was so much to remind me,' he said at last.

'Aye, well I'm back now and I don't have many stories. It wasn't all it was cracked up to be and it was too hot. They wanted blood, mate. They weren't happy unless I was sweating it . . .'

Mackie checked himself. There was a silence between them. Then he said,

'Do you think he knew anything about it?'

'They said he wouldn't have. They said it was quick, all over in a flash.'

'Jesus, I was just joking,' said Mackie. 'All those things I said to him. I was scared for him but really I was just pissing about.'

'It doesn't matter,' said Drew. 'He wouldn't have had it any different. I took him to the station the last time. He was well up for it.'

'What about Mel?' asked Mackie.

'She's surviving,' Drew said. 'I met her last night. You know she broke up with him just before.'

'I heard,' said Mackie. 'But they'd have got back together. They always did.'

'I said that to her. She said I was probably right. I think she just needed a break from the pressure of him being there. We should go to The Thistle for a beer. I promised him. There's a lock-in tonight. Dougie told me.'

'Aye,' said Mackie. 'A pint for old time's sake.'

After Drew turned off the TV, before they got to the door, he grabbed Mackie's arm and stopped him.

'Listen, mate,' he said. 'It sounds stupid but this morning something happened.'

Mackie looked at him.

'What?' he asked.

Drew shook his head.

'Something weird, a feeling.'

'Scottie?'

Drew nodded his head.

'If he's anywhere he'll be at The Thistle.'

Drew grinned.

'Aye,' he said. 'Come on.'

Scottie thought about following them down, thought about how that would turn out, but when he reached the back yard his mind fell on the girl instead. He kept Drew and Mackie's voices in his head as he made his way out of there, his feet crunching on ice. He was not wandering aimlessly anymore. His steps had a purpose. The army had taught him how to have purpose, taught him about direction and meaning. In the confusion he'd lost his purpose but now it was back. He felt energised by it. He wanted to see the girl, wanted to show her a different side to him. He thought about what might have happened if she'd not been there, if she'd not helped him. He thought about being lost, about wandering around in the darkness forever. He thought about the things he'd said to her and all of the things he was going to say as he made his way down Hillside to the cemetery gates, his legs carrying him onward, the ice glistening under the street lights.

The night was crystal clear. There were a million stars in the sky and a million more beyond. He craned his neck to look at them as he walked, remembering nights just like this in the war zone, remembering the barrack roof, remembering Atkinson and his stories, remembering the looter in the street. A chill ran through him but he chased it away. There was no more going back.

There was no border to the garden either. He simply came upon it. One moment he was in the cemetery and the next it was there in front of him. Looking back he could not see where he had come from, could not see Hillside or the lights of the estate. There was only the garden. The ice had disappeared, the bitter chill with it. The garden was set in springtime, the leaves green and fresh, blossom on the branches, new growth everywhere, buds opening, the smell of flowers, the trickle of water, the sun warm on his face, insects dancing. He walked amongst them, unsure of himself, of where to step, feeling he had reached a place he was meant to be but not knowing what to do now that he was there. He noticed a stone wall covered in ivy, went to it, found a spot and sat. Part of him still ached. There was no denying it, but the aching was tempered now and the aching wasn't physical. A feeling of belonging was growing inside of him, nudging its way into the places where the feeling of being lost had festered, pressing against the guilt, ushering those feelings away. It made a difference. He had a place now, a place to rest.

The girl appeared out of nowhere. She was smiling. She sat down next to him on the wall and took his hand in hers. There was warmth in her touch, nothing like the feeling he'd had when he touched his mother's face. This was not something remembered. It was real. He sensed his uncle somewhere close by, others too, their familiarity.

'Are you ready?' she asked.

He nodded.

'It's for the best,' she said. 'Believe me.'

'I believe you,' he said. 'Let's go.'

A multitude of feelings washed over him, the weirdest sensations, a great burden relinquishing its grip, the pain from his shoulder diminishing to nothing, hunger, thirst, worries flowing away, insecurities pouring from his being, a cleansing.

It was like floating or swimming under water.

It was like swimming under water but not having to worry about drawing a breath.

It was like being something other than human.

The End

Acknowledgements

I started writing *Soldier Boy* in the summer of 2004, not knowing if the conflicts in Iraq and Afghanistan would still be relevant issues by the time the book was completed. At the time of writing, both conflicts continue.

I would like to thank the following organisations and individuals for their help and support in the completion of this novel:

The Society of Authors, The Authors' Foundation and the K. Blundell Trust Award – Mark Armory, Sir Michael Holroyd, Gary McKeone, Ruth Scurr, Ali Smith and Paula Johnson.

All at The Maia Press.

Karolina Sutton and Laura Sampson at Curtis Brown.

Mark Williams, Jim Birt, Jerry Vyse and John McHenry for photographs and inspiration. Sorry I couldn't use everything.

Justin Stone, David Wilson, Bruce Partleton and Dani Simmons for advice, observations, feedback and, in the latter case, expertise.

Callum Hobson. Good luck in your chosen career.

David Couch for the website.

Rachel and Morgan, for their patience, love and laughter.

The music of Bruce Springsteen (particularly the albums *Devils and Dust*, *The Rising* and *Magic*), Tom McRae (*All Maps Welcome*), The Arcade Fire (*Funeral*), Kate Bush (*Aerial*), Neil Young (*Living with War*), Midlake (*The Trials of Van Occupanther*), The Waterboys (*Universal Hall*), Bright Eyes (*Cassadagia*) and Sun Volt (*The Search*).

Finally, I would like to direct the reader to the story of Royal Highland Fusilier Private Gordon Gentle, which prompted me to write this novel.

Visit my website at www.dannyrhodes.net.

Danny Rhodes
ASBOVILLE

£8.99   ISBN 978 1 904559 22 1

**'A-S-B-O. You think that
makes you special. But it
doesn't. It means you were
stupid enough to get caught,
that's all.'**

When sixteen-year-old JB is
served with an ASBO, he is sent
to live with his uncle on the
coast to paint beach huts. It's
a chance for him to turn his
life around, but as the summer
days drag by, JB's feelings of
frustration and isolation grow.
Only his tentative relationship
with Sal offers any chance of
rescue. But a storm is coming that threatens to shatter his hopes and
destroy the relationship that could redeem him.

'Moving and atmospheric, a coming-of-age tale with political bite'
   Guardian

'Sure sense of pace and keen evocation of seaside life' *Observer*

'A coming-of-age story with an actually rather shy, sensitive and
   likeable kid as its hero' *Independent on Sunday*

'Rhodes asks important questions about social justice, but also tells
   a compelling human story. An impressive debut' *New Statesman*

'A finely crafted and often lyrical debut novel which offers far more
   than hoodie-hugging sympathy or sink-estate despair'
   Independent

'An excellent debut novel, definitely in my top ten of the year'
   Bookseller

Kolton Lee THE LAST CARD

£8.99   ISBN 978 1 904559 25 2

H is a boxer past his prime. Haunted by the memory of the fight that should have made him great, he is chasing his dream through the seedier side of the London boxing circuit. A gunfight at an illegal gambling shebeen drags him into an underworld of violence and extortion, and H finds himself in debt to a sinister sociopath. Once and for all he must face his demons and enter the ring one final time. A striking thriller – authentic, revelatory, fast-moving and entertaining.

'A simmering *noir* novel . . . sweaty, brutal and powerful' *Observer*

'Impressive debut . . . Lee serves up spot-on dialogue . . . a thrilling new twist in an unusual setting' *Guardian*

'He cranks up the tension and keeps it simmering . . . reveals a London we are all fascinated by but are scared to tread' Alex Wheatle

Dreda Say Mitchell RUNNING HOT

£8.99   ISBN 978 1 904559 09 2

What's the best thing about Hackney? The bus outta here! Elijah 'Schoolboy' Campbell has just seven days to get out of a London underworld where bling, ringtones and petty deaths are accessories of life. Schoolboy knows that when you're running hot all it takes is one call, one voicemail, one text to disconnect you from this life – permanently. Dreda Say Mitchell perfectly captures the tough and brittle mood of inner London in this stark, moving and funny debut novel.

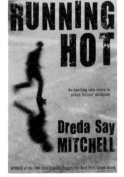

'An exciting new voice in urban fiction' *Guardian*
'Swaggeringly cool and incredibly funny' *Stirling Observer*
'Very sharp' *Sunday Telegraph* 'Taut and exhilarating' *Tribune*
'Fast-moving, colourfully written' *Times Literary Supplement*
'Distinctly different . . . well worth seeking out' *Literary Review*
WINNER OF THE CWA JOHN CREASEY DAGGER FOR BEST FIRST CRIME NOVEL